Love Stories
of The
Central Coast

Additional copies may be ordered from the publisher for educational, business, promotional or premium use.
For information, contact ALIVE Book Publishing at:
alivebookpublishing.com

Book design by Alex P. Johnson

ISBN 13
978-1-63132-264-8 Paperback

Library of Congress Control Number: 2025920290

Library of Congress Cataloging-in-Publication Data
is available upon request.

First Edition

Published in the United States of America by ALIVE Book Publishing
an imprint of Advanced Publishing LLC
3200 A Danville Blvd., Suite 204, Alamo, California 94507
alivebookpublishing.com

PRINTED IN THE UNITED STATES OF AMERICA

10 9 8 7 6 5 4 3 2 1

Love Stories
of The
Central Coast

T. Garner Edwards

Alive Book Publishing

*For Jacqueline Cunningham Edwards,
for a lifetime of great love,
not to mention all the honest
editorial feedback to my writing
(and all else!) over the years.*

Acknowledgments

To fellow writers, Helen, Susan, Deanna, Bill, and Jackie for their ideas and encouragement related to this work.

To friends, Tristan, Rosie, and Stacia for their encouragement and invaluable feedback on my stories.

To my wife, Jackie, for sorting through my many photos of Carmel Beach and bringing two of them to life for the front and back covers of this book.

Contents

A Fresh Baked Pie

Walking through my rows of trees bulging with apples always brought me great satisfaction, but on this morning as I strode through the orchard, my subconscious began signaling, as if attempting to warn me of an as yet unrecognized problem. Thinking this lethargy might be mitigated by an early morning nap, I interrupted my inspection of the repairs to the irrigation system and headed home. Suddenly, as I stepped into a clearing and saw my house on the horizon, I stopped. It had been a while since I ventured beyond my land to hunt and explore the forests. I always came awake in the wilds. I smiled recalling those winsome romantic adventures from which something always might have, but never had, happened. The whys and the regrets brought a pang to my heart, strong sporadic histories extending interims over years diminishing hope for meaningful affection. The idea of investigating an answer created resolve. I packed a lunch and headed for the field house to get my hiking pack and rifle.

Coyotes caused problems among ranchers in our area, as well as in most every other. I have had success keeping them off my ranch. One always carried calls and looked for prints and scat, but on this day I would not be sitting and waiting half an hour to take out some *canis latrans*. I intended to move higher to where my land mingled with heavy foliage and other people's properties. Along the way, one could get a squirrel or a rabbit or a fox, always fair game as a destroyer, if so inclined.

I passed the edge of my spread into a cove of trees,

Douglas fir, western red cedar, western hemlock, Sitka spruce nestled between two hills leading away from several private ranches. These old forests ran thick and noisy with questions, always new, by a different bird, a moving deer, a creaking tree, a scampering animal, or occasionally a lumbering bear, and less frequently in waiting a cougar, wanting to see how you would act on what you may or may not have heard, always something to learn. I have been entertained by squirrels and raccoons running across the tops of the trees depending on the time of year. They have thrown branches and pinecones and laughed themselves silly, with me ducking as they snickered to one another. Sometimes quiet near silence but always interrupted by a woodpecker hack-hack-hacking, or by the wind twisting and swishing, or by the falling of an eagle or the jumping of an owl flapping its wings through the upper branches. Sometimes it would be an unknown cause, and I would prepare to defend myself or my dog, although on this day I no longer had my faithful Wrecker, who had passed quite naturally some weeks before. I knew how to use a rifle. As long as I stayed alert observing, I would generally have the advantage against animals. I had no fear of them or of dying. Living and enjoying living would always be my first choice, at least until I get too old to know the difference, still a ways off according to my current skills of rumination.

I never found a woman of my dreams who came to both love me and live with me. I had great friends who were women. We enjoyed each other. Mostly, they chose me about the same as I chose them. One of them I did love, but we never got married. The woman I spent the most time with over the past ten years recently passed. We used to keep each other from getting too lonely. I said a lot of heartfelt words at her funeral, eighteen months back. Her kids call me Jonesy. I help them whenever I can.

I made a lot of choices. Good decisions mean I have a successful ranch, raise a lot of livestock, sell a lot of apples, earn a lot of money, am a productive member of the community, and then there are those others I wish I could take back. I find myself thinking about what I have thought about before and how there may be no way to fix what I cannot fix, because if I could, I would have fixed it when it should have been fixed.

After about an hour and a half, I finally reached the clearing near the ridge of the two hills that formed the cove. I crawled over boulders and different rock formations. I had been here before, often. I knew where to go so I could see anybody's property. I headed toward one of my favorite high spots on the other side of the ridge. I edged my foot onto a root growing out of the dirt and eased myself to the top. I barely had my balance when I heard the click of a rifle.

"Hold it right there, Mr. Jones. It seems I've got the jump on you again."

I thought, how exasperating. "Sasha, I appreciate your sense of humor. But that rife makes me nervous."

I heard the rifle click again. I turned. Her face surrounded by white hair captured qualities I admired. Natural, honest, fair, in her own way so beautiful I actually gasped a little, and you could tell another thing had not changed. She did not take any shit from anybody.

"What're you doing on my land?" Her voice sounded serious, but with the lilt of a tease.

"We haven't even seen each other for quite some time."

"And?"

"And I just thought I'd go for a hike, and well, I might have secretly planned on talking to you."

Sasha pushed her hand against my pack. "You probably have nothing to eat but those ridiculous hiking rations." She walked ahead. When I hesitated a moment because her civility had taken me aback, she turned. "Well, are you coming? I figured you'd want the bluff overlooking my land."

"That is one of my favorite views," I said.

I followed her through the boulders above her property on the northwestern section. You could see Mount Baker topped with glaciers far to the north.

"You want to pick your spot?" she asked.

"No, I want you to pick your spot first."

She studied me. She looked at the nearby forested hills and the view of the river gorges leading to the white peaks and the clear blue sky, then she shrugged and sat near where I might also be able to find a comfortable place to decry the panoramic valleys and the majestic mountains.

I pulled a bag from my jacket. "I made a sandwich this morning before I left. Subconscious volition leaned on coming up here to maybe see you even if I hadn't allowed myself to admit it kind of influenced how I put everything together. I'd like to split it with you. It's kind of special. I think you'll like it."

She nodded appreciatively. "You know, Jones, sometimes you use a lot of words. Got anything to drink?"

"Water."

"In a bottle?"

"Of course it's in a bottle, no Cal, just water."

She smiled. "Okay."

I handed her half the sandwich followed by the water, and from my shirt a napkin.

"Thank you." She nodded as if she were especially impressed by the napkin. "Jones, what're you coming up here for today?"

How many times had I had this conversation in my own head, and how would I make this time different? I had put in hours, days, weeks, months of thinking, and I still had not come up with anything good.

"I wanted to see you. There's so many times over the years...and now as we're both alone, I'm just wondering."

"Could be people end up alone by choice?"

"That is true. I do know how true that is."

"I know you do, Jones. You along with many others, including me."

"I've enjoyed all the, I could call them, escapades, yours and mine? We have discovered ourselves, coincidentally, in the same forest hunting the same stag. And about how when we have come, coincidentally, across each other doing so many other things so often every few weeks it seems, months here and there, year after year, and all the same interests, same jobs, meeting the same people, when we have been so fond of each other for so long, even having a laugh..."

"That's true." She nodded as if to confirm every word.

I hoped for an open embrace to my words. "I care so much about you. I have missed you over the years." I have no idea why I started in on the past. I made sure I stopped before I went too far. "I think you should let us have a chance here, near the ends of our lives. You know...you know how I feel about you."

Sasha rocked back and forth on the granite boulder as if she had to take a respectful moment for reflection. She scanned the imposing slopes of her ranch. She shielded her face from the eastern sun. She took another glance at the white topped northern volcano, almost as if to see if it still brought her calm. "I have to get some work done." The words sounded like a death knoll gliding along the wind. She took the last bite of her sandwich and handed me the wrapper. I stuck it in my pocket.

"Good sandwich, Jones."

"I'm a good cook," I said finally. "I can cook you some fine meals."

"There was a time. We had a time. I have reflected about how it would have been, even contemplated how it would be now and again. I like you, and what's more, I have always liked you and I have even loved you." She sighed deeply. "Some of me still does."

"Well, then..." It almost sounded as if I were begging. "You know where I came from?"

"California."

"And I left..."

"Because you couldn't afford it."

"I can now. I've been thinking of going back. Still have a family home in Carmel."

"Of course, I'd miss you, Jones. That goes without saying."

"I want you to come with me."

She gripped her rifle and stood.

"We could go back and forth. I want you by my side."

Slowly, she lifted her face to mine, as if she needed to study every molecule beneath my offer. "I could bake you a pie and you could come by for dessert sometime..." Her voice simply trailed away.

At least she had offered something. I nudged her with my head. "I want you to be with me, and that's more than a fresh baked pie."

She gave me a hug with one hand. We stared into each other's eyes long enough for me to know she had heard and considered my words. She knew what I wanted. She smiled and turned away. Then she looked back. "Tomorrow night at seven. Don't be late."

My heart about leapt through my chest, as I watched Sasha shuffle and slide down the cliff toward her ranch, killing it like a pro.

The Start of Something Big

Near the end of the shift on April 23, 1906, the number of city-blocks cleared of rubble concerned him not. He would keep going as long as the money kept coming. One of the other workers hollered, 'That's block thirty-two!' Karl just laughed. He had no regrets. Every day, like now, he had breathed lingering smoke and smelled the onslaught of other noisome sensations. He thought *noisome* a funny word. It said one thing and meant another. No mask could protect olfactory cognition. His mother had taught him lot of big words. He knew that meant understanding smells. He could distinguish a gamut of pungent differences, including carcasses, buildings, asphalt, and burned up artifacts. On this day unstable liquid earth had grabbed at his boots, as if to dare him to walk across compost piles of building rubble to reach pockets of interrupted walkways and blocked carriage drives. He ran through wreckage with ease. Nobody questioned a working boy strong enough to stack heavy building chunks, especially when this city of opportunity had been so completely demolished by earthquake and conflagration. Karl shook his head as he worked toward where he would receive his pay. He respected and feared fire consumption, as he brushed past what used to be department stores, now black hunks of brick and cement jutting up in jagged columns from ash heaps here and there. He pretended they froze while reaching toward the sun and their former glory. He considered the power of locomotives, having ridden behind so many on his way to the Pacific's Central Coast. It shocked him to see them toppled. They lay effetely on their sides with feet sticking out, their dynamics stolen by Mother Nature. Effete, what his father used to call men who couldn't fight, it seemed to apply to trains unable to run or even stand. He had stepped on heavy steel tracks over which wheels so smoothly used to roll, now twisted like rubber, no longer ensured rounded surfaces for flowing whirling grooves. In many places it looked as if God himself had ripped apart the earth. Karl visualized giant hands gripping, stretching, contorting roads and buildings, and unseen lips blowing gales of fire across the sky propelling hefty chunks of every-thing through the air, caverns, flame, smoke blocking access, smothering trucks, cars, cows, and people, so much damage, so much heat, so much panic. Karl absorbed this scene. He belonged here. Disaster had given him a home.

He scraped caked scum from his fingers and got in line. After the foreman doled out his pay, he headed out with purpose. As a worker, each day he received the promised minimum of a dollar twenty-seven for a nine-hour shift. In addition, they gave him other morsels to keep energy pro-ductive throughout the day, and he always tucked away some of that for the other two under his care. Now, he made his way to where he desired, because of a particular person he thought he would like to know.

He gave a polite nod to the young woman and placed ten pennies on the counter of the small shack, Hoffman Cafe, with dark stained construction-grade siding, like a midsized closet beneath a wood-shingled roof. "I'd like two or three of any type of rolls or bread you have left and a cup of milk, if you please."

That morning while shoveling debris, he had seen the same girl at the same cafe counter, which is why he decided to choose a bit of a circuity on his route back to feed the twins. *Circuity*, a word his mother used when he didn't give her a straight answer.

The girl wore a small brimmed cap. It caused her brownish blond hair to poof out just a bit over her ears. Now her pale blue eyes studied him with curiosity.

Closer in, he looked younger than he had from a distance. "You don't have to pay. We're givin' food away."

The dancing tones of her voice affected him even more enticingly than he had imagined. He celebrated his courage to have taken the chance to make her acquaintance. The world seemed to be suddenly opening up. Her reaction to him lifted his hopes and gave him promise of at least a gentle connection. He regarded her more closely. He needed to determine what she meant exactly. She could not think him a beggar. He had earned that ten cents. His presence covered from head to toe in soot and cement dust proved as much. "Been working all day hauling rubble so as to make a good impression on the likes of you, in case next time, like maybe something happens, and I don't have anything to buy food with for a little boy and girl who I'm looking after and taking food to right now."

The young woman tilted her head, his face so young. She considered, maybe sixteen. His attitude seemed older. Thin, but muscular, he had arms and shoulders big and broad. Also, of little concern to her, but she couldn't help but notice his handsomeness. She imagined him lifting some heavy cemented rocks and bricks and debris and heaving them as far as most anybody. As a result of what he'd been doing all day, he looked filthy and he smelled a little, kind of like burned cabbage. "You bring me a fresh bucket of water from the fountain yonder, and we're square." She handed Karl two empty buckets.

Karl had not considered this as an option. He looked around for a water spigot. "Is the water running down here yet?"

The girl shook her head. He noticed her hair hardly moved. Her skin seemed smooth and clean. She relaxed her voice, it came out low and reassuring. "Hasn't gotten this far yet. S'posed to be tomorrow or the next day."

He could hardly think. "You know, miss, I don't have to get water. I have money to pay for some food."

She barely moved. He let her capture his attention again. Seeing her expression, something to behold, nearly took the wind right out of him. She smiled as if she were his sister or a close friend, thinking so it seemed, not so much about him, but more specifically what might be good for him. She turned away. He followed her focus to a bar of soap behind the counter.

"I need some water, and ..." she looked him up and down. "So do you."

Golly. She probably thought he smelled. Piece by piece, Karl passed over the bags of food he had collected for the twins. He kept his attention on her as she moved, as he figured he had a right to do until she had placed his last bag under the counter. She looked up expectantly at him.

"I'll make it as quick as I can," he said.

Karl strode toward Golden Gate Park where he knew they always had water. It meant a long traverse. He hoped before he got there, he would come upon running municipal pipes already repaired by the Spring Valley Water Company. Now at five days, repaired pipes did serve a few neighborhoods here and there throughout the city.

Charging ahead, Karl observed the people, rich, poor, different backgrounds and races putting their shoulders together using hands, muscles, horses, pulleys, hammers, ropes, cables, carriages, carts, engines, and everything else to make it easier and safer for citizens to wind their way through the four-and-a-half square miles of rubble that used to be San Francisco. Suddenly, he stopped when he saw a water spigot sticking up from a garden.

He turned it on.

No water came out.

He reminded himself, no one to blame but himself for choosing to keep his money and not pay the young woman. But then he thought, how stupid, because she said he didn't even have to pay, which caused some confusion. Then he encouraged himself with the most peculiar reflection, perhaps she just wanted him to get water so he could clean himself up. He had worked long hours every day. He felt the dollars in his pocket. He knew he would meet his goal of freedom and food and shelter, but that didn't make him clean. Now, as he neared the park, the young woman's visage appeared crystal clear in his head, an earthshaking reminiscence, two or three years older and therefore probably not much interested in the likes of him.

In Golden Gate Park a long line of men doing exactly the same waited with empty buckets in hand. Everyone kept moving, so it didn't take long before he quick stepped it back toward the Hoffman Cafe. Karl wondered about the words he had seen on the side of the Hoffman Cafe: "Eat, Drink and Be Merry, for Tomorrow We May Have to Go to Oakland." He thought it showed a mean streak toward the people of Oakland. He wondered if the pretty girl had anything to do with that.

He still had plenty of strength in his legs. Even at his quickened pace, he had not spilled a drip over the lip of either of the full buckets of water. The sun had begun to escape, and he needed to get to Gregory and Glenna.

Karl noticed the young woman already had her eye on him. He wondered how long she had been watching him. She had a basket on the counter filled with his food bags. She seemed receptive. "What is it?" he asked.

"Some things," she said. "You haven't told me your name."

"Karl. And yours?"

"Sarah."

"Nice to meet you, Sarah."

"Nice to meet you, Karl. I was thinking about you and your brother and sister, how maybe you might be able to spend the night in a real place."

"How do you know we ain't in a real place?"

Sarah smiled, "I don't. Are you in a real place?"

Now Karl smiled. "No ma'am. We're sort of in some broken down building with some hiding places in the middle."

"I asked my Pa. He said you could bring your brother and sister along."

Karl studied her again, this time to see what lay behind her suggestion. "We gonna be safe?"

She didn't answer. Her look told him she didn't think she needed to answer. Her eyes filled with warmth and trust, even hope, like when new young orphans first entered the orphanage, before they learned the truth of how their lives would change.

"I'm not going to answer that question. It's just whatever you think," she said. "Also, there isn't enough difference in age for you to be calling me *ma'am*."

He had been fooled by people before, but she looked so sincere. Her last comment pretty much gave him clarity.

She wanted him to make his own conclusions without her having to say any more about it. "I think you're a good person."

"I am."

"So, I'll do it. Even though I've learned there aren't many I can trust. Also, they aren't any relation, they're not my brother and sister. They're orphans, twins to each other, and now probably wondering where I am. We all used to live in the same place before the quake."

"You used to live in an orphanage?"

Momentarily, grief overcame him. He took a deep breath. He had aligned so much of himself with his parents. They made life magnificent. Their deaths changed his world. He regained control and nodded. He shrugged and scrunched his mouth. "Killed in a storm. Swept away by raging floods." He looked back at Sarah.

"I'm sorry," said Sarah.

Karl nodded without comment.

Sarah touched his arm. He did not respond. She opened the back door to the cafe.

"Here. First, fill two thermoses. Then, use the rest of the water with soap. Take your time. Clean towel here on the door to dry off. And one of my father's old shirts, but fresh."

Karl hadn't used soap and water for a few days. As he bathed, she boarded up the cafe's window. That gave him privacy to clean more places. He realized the importance of looking presentable. He would keep that in mind and even change his clothes when he went to find a serious job. He centered the towel over the hook on the back of the door. For a moment he observed the thick construction wood forming the walls of the little washing shack, before he stepped outside.

He watched her look him over, as if she were the official inspector.

"The only reason I survived. They tossed me up on a balcony."

"Thank God for that," said Sarah. She handed him the basket and took the two thermoses and placed them in the folds of her overcoat.

He felt self-conscious, as for the longest time she did not remove her eyes from his. A pang, a wish, an ethereal whisper, he sensed anxiety, promise, and risk. From her, he wanted acceptance and warmth.

He leaned in close enough to kiss her.

After a moment she took his hand.

Remember Joni Mitchell?

Again, I drove by the Carmel cottage I once had the pleasure of knowing, the place now long unoccupied.

The wooden garage carries decades of neglect, a somber burden. Windows boarded over and missing shingles lighten the dark whip-scratched exterior. A flap of stiff black roofing paper clings patched and forgotten near the corner closest to the outside lamp missing panes of glass. A broken stake fence lumbering parallel to the street stumbles cut in half by a dry rotted door held together by rusty nails and hinges. It would not swing so much as scrape, tilt, and object if released from the latch.

No flowers bloom within the fenced area alongside the garage across the entire property. No camellias, no poppies, no Mexican sage welcome hummingbirds into alluring sweet nectar. No honeysuckle and no fruit trees yield enough energy to smile and listen to honeybees singing their buzzing songs celebrating in so many ways over so many days so many years ago. Only a dry unkept collection of distressed plants, little more than aspiring sticks, foretell what may lay beyond the expansive non-fragrant hedge.

I do not follow overgrown weeds along the irregular stone path to the patio, still shielded from the street, secret privacy of neglect and loss, I am sure, instead of high energy expectations in vibrant hues intermingling with inspiring garden fragrances.

No brightly colored hanging plants with a myriad of styles enrich my visions. No artistic ceramic pots and vases filled with festive perennials shouting out their personalities to the invitee. No place settings, nor candles nor accoutrements nor bouquets demand enthusiasm for being!

No young woman with flowing big hair and piercing blue eyes smiles and gently waves a hand, holding a peanut in front of her as she catches the attention of a blue bird on the limb of a nearby cypress tree. And no blue bird glides through the air with confidence and faith landing on those extended, delicate fingers. No blue bird holds a smooth and natural nail with its claws while exchanging glances with the kind human before taking the peanut and fluttering to a nearby potted plant to peck-peck-peck bury below the surface of the tended garden soil the peanut, preserved for a later treat.

No singing with Joni Mitchell in the background "I could drink a case of you."

* * *

"What have you been thinking about?"

I look up and see an elderly woman sitting near and studying me. I take in the moment. "About someone I once knew."

"Oh, who would that be?"

I step toward her. I bend down and look into her piercing blue eyes.

We kiss.

"Who else, but you?"

The Building Code

Rosie held the photo of her one great love, Robert, husband, grandad, lover, protector, provider. She squeezed the glass and pushed his image against her lips and looked across the view of Monterey Bay they had shared so many times over a cup of coffee. She left the house, walked across the deck and through the backyard to the basement. She would often continue to her art studio, but on this morning she opened the four by five-foot door, carefully positioned her feet on the homemade redwood steps outside and inside, flipped on the light and scanned the white waterproofed cement floors, the hand-crafted bookcases supported with triangular Monterey pine scraps and extending along one wall, the two large work benches on wheels near the opposite wall of hanging tools and odds and ends, the storage area beyond with neatly stacked bins for fifty-one years of every holiday season, and file cabinets with writings and artifacts and unfinished plans for thousands of other writings, inventions, and musical ideas. She joked sadly to herself, *Where was Granddad when she needed him?* She knew all too well. Stacks of lumber bits sat in three different places. Small indoor pieces filled several drawers. Longer two by fours with partial sheets of plywood of various thicknesses and other indoor wood sat underneath the black writing-music table. Longer larger rough pieces hung from posts past the shelves containing paint cans through the full-sized basement door that led to the dry ground and water drainage system underneath the house.

One by one, Rosie took the pieces of wood by the writing table and set each by size and shape outside on the ground bark in front of the art studio. She had a few two-by-twos three or four feet long, several two-by-fours between two and six feet in length, and various widths of plywood of different thicknesses. To get to the wood underneath the house, she had to avoid hanging insulation, cross beneath four-inch black drainage pipes, walk around one set of shelves to reach another, while avoiding a series of old phone cables, all the while hoping not to turn an ankle or stumble over the lumpy earthen floor. She found two or three pieces she might want to use. Two she made note of. One she carried, beneath the wires, under the pipe, twirling it around the other set of shelves without hitting the small hot water heater and the exterior of the basement wall, then bending down to get underneath the second drainage pipe, before lifting the wood high enough not to knock over one of the paint cans on her way back through the door to the basement. In all the years she had lived with Robert in this house, she had never shuffled below the floor joists and braces along the lumpy earth under the house. Robert would have been the one to do it. She might have suggested it to him. For a moment her perceptions swelled from loneliness. Now, it had become her responsibility to do the building, whatever that meant, she would do her part to make things right.

She sketched with pencil and paper what she had in mind to build. She examined the pieces of wood she had laid on the bark to see what parts of her design to manage. She marked where to cut pieces of the wood, as she had seen him do. She had never used his saws and some of the other tools. She liked finding his zone. She had confidence she could do it. She had worked the Dremel and the sander, the drill and the screwdriver. The newness of organizing pieces of wood into elements and creating the parts so they could be attached with glue and screws alerted her hopeful nature.

The art studio had a mini outdoor workbench. She intended to use that to cut scraps of wood into pieces. As for the longer boards, she thought she might have to set up the workhorses. She placed them a few feet apart and spanned them with the two longest two-by-fours covered with plywood to make a platform. She called on Robert's presence. "How do you like this?" she asked. She laughed to herself. "I'm about to use your circular saw. I hope I don't lose any fingers. And I'll keep the cord behind me."

She had seen Robert plug an extension cord into the art studio and the basement depending on where he needed access for the saw. Rosie discovered the basement plugs did not always work. One was attached to a circuit controlled by the light switch, one was controlled by the switch on one of the work benches, and one was on a wall plug with multiple attached outlets that had to be held steady while inserting the plug as it moved back and forth. She decided to trust what she knew best, the professionally installed outlets in her art studio.

The first time she squeezed the trigger of the circular saw, it caught her by surprise by jumping in the air. Quickly, Rosie set it down. It had come within inches of taking a bite out of her leg. She gathered calm, as she noticed a guard protector had popped around the blade. She rededicated herself to her goal, with purpose. She improved her ability to cut by keeping the saw flat with steady pressure.

Later she found a jigsaw for corners and smaller pieces. As long as she moved with patience and firmness, she could adjust ways to cut so finished pieces fit snugly together. Using Robert's tools and materials was like absorbing a little of him.

As she worked to find the right drill to make a hole so the screw would hold and not split the wood, Rosie reminisced about Robert, when they met, when he proposed, the day he pretended to just want to eat ice cream, as she pretended she had not seen him leaning against the tree staring at her. Always teasing each other, playing tricks and feigning disagreements then consoling and showing each other how much they meant to each other, she suspected something. Finally, casually, Robert sauntered toward her and knelt in front of the bench where she was sitting. The look of sincerity on his face as he proposed caused her to pretend faint and fall on top of him. As her head landed on his shoulder, she whispered, "Since I love you so much, I guess I will." He laughed. She laughed, and he wrapped his arms around her.

Now everything she had made she set outside on the redwood deck. When the doorbell rang, she walked through the laundry room and opened the garage door.

Gerald ran across the driveway into Grammy's arms.

"Hi, Grammy, I love you!"

"I love you too, Ger."

The four-year-old held Grammy's legs, as if she were a life raft in the deep end. She leaned down and kissed his head. She patted him on the back.

The little boy dug his face harder into Grammy's knees. "I miss Granddad."

Grammy empathized with Gerald's sadness. "I miss Granddad, too."

Steven, the tall bearded son-in-law, carried a sleeping bag and a backpack with a lunchbox. "He didn't eat as much as usual this morning."

"Okay. How are you doing, Steven?"

"Good, although tomorrow's flight to Boston got moved up to 6 a.m. How are you coming along, Rosie"

"I'm alright. That's really early. Care for a cup of coffee?"

"Love to, but I have a lot of preparation for the trip."

"Another time then. You have a good day," said Rosie.

"You too. Hug good-bye, Ger-Bear?"

Gerald stretched his arms. Steven lifted him for a long hug. "See you soon, Ger. I love you."

"I love you, dad," said Ger.

Grammy closed the garage door and opened the side door into the house.

"Shoes off," said Grammy. Grammy and Gerald removed their shoes.

As usual, Gerald ran into the bedroom with the toys. Grammy sorted through the backpack and set the used lunch box and other items needing to be washed into the sink. She tossed clothes wrapped in the new bedroll into the washer and placed whatever did not need to be washed on the dining room table. Gerald conformed to his typical pattern of spending quite a bit of time with the toys he had not seen for two weeks. When Rosie looked in on him, he did not notice her. She returned to the kitchen to prepare a snack and to see with anticipation what Gerald would bring from the bedroom to play with. To her surprise, Gerald chose no basket of play toys. Instead, he came running down the hall crying while cuddling Greenie, the favorite teddy.

Grammy lifted Gerald and he sank into her arms. "What's the matter, Ger?"

"Grammy, I had a really bad week at pre-school."

"Oh, Ger, I'm sorry to hear that. Do you want to talk about it?"

Ger sobbed even harder, "No."

Grammy rocked Gerald back and forth. "Everybody has a bad week once in a while."

Ger lifted his face while he cried. "But mine was *really* bad!"

Grammy's heart ached. She let Gerald continue to cry. "There, there, we will figure something out." She walked to where she could see the back deck through the family room door. When Gerald finally began to wind down, she held him away from her so he could see her face. "Did you know, sometimes Granddad had a bad week."

"Granddad?"

"That's right."

"I didn't know that."

"Even when he was a little kid, like you. He told me all kinds of stories from his childhood."

"Sometimes Granddad had a bad week?"

"So when I heard you had a bad week, I thought, what would Granddad do? What do you think he would have done?"

"I don't know," said Gerald.

"So I went into Granddad's shop, and I thought of what Granddad did when he had a bad week, like make something good, and then he would feel better, so that's what I did."

She opened the door to the back deck. Gerald could see a wooden garage with places for many Hot Wheels to park, and blocks of wood with ramps that could be positioned different ways. A new car sat at the top of one ramp waiting for someone to let it rush to the bottom. "Grammy, let me down, let me down."

"OK," said Grammy.

"Here," said Gerald. He handed off Greenie.

Rosie took it. She watched Gerald run to what she had made for him. His excitement and joy filled her with love. She looked across the yard towards Santa Cruz over the expansive bay with scores of sailboats full of wind, riding over white caped waves. She smiled. She could feel Robert had been watching her, as if wondering what had taken her so long to finally start building what she had always suggested he should do.

Clarity of Critical Thinking Re: Love

The haze clarifying hard perceptions became more and less and more and less dense and never cleared or went away anymore. She had requested her bed be moved toward the ocean pounding against the jagged rocks lining a Highlands cove rising from the private beach from which she had strolled and perennially contemplated life's reflections. She turned her head so she could see. Gentle heaving and pushing of some truths never tempted a final calling. Falling and rising, dimming and glowing and living, tripping, washing and celebrating, crying, longing and thrilling...having the universalness of exceptional character innate in all known and unknown stories so no dears would ever fret about relevance of their perceived love.

At twenty she had considered two men out of any number of potentials. They looked so alike, and in manner they could have been brothers, both so brilliant and charming, six feet tall, penetrating eyes, strong and athletic, quick thinking and confident. Both officers, during the war, she could see each on leave, as fortune would have it, taking a break from the fighting and danger, never at the same time. She wondered if either would not return home. One asked her to marry. The other took her to his suite the night before a very dangerous assignment. This one had a unique aspect, unimagined pheromones so appealing to her sense, somehow influencing her toward an anomalous indiscretion becoming the first and only time she had enjoyed such intense physical pleasure, so surprising, it twisted the logic she had so carefully annotated about behaviors before the wedding night to say nothing about what made a good husband and father.

Subsequently, a villain thrust its overwhelming power into the equation, an untimely and earth-shattering end to life. Tormented by Death having crawled into battle and stolen that man, she became crazy and inconsolable. After mere days of suffering, the other man arrived on leave and he too wanted to marry, his love so rich, as he said, in case and before something bad might happen to him. He had no awareness of what she had just endured. Even if she did not have the same attraction to him as she had discovered for the other, she did feel a kind of agape love. With the promise of his love for her, she would create a solid union with someone for whom she had strong feelings and so much in common. They wed and they honeymooned for two days before he was gone again, back to war leaving her wondering whether he would also be a valued temptation for Death.

Pregnancy brought fine celebrations. Secretly, she thought the glowing nature of the shared time with the first man more likely caused inception than the thoughtful caring and considerate shared time with her husband. As she raised her son, she always thought of whom she considered his father, a consideration never communicated to anyone. Her husband came home at the end of the war. He exemplified how to be a good father to this son, who copied everything who he thought was his real father did, and so they grew to have a complete, respectful, and loving father-son relationship.

Often she reflected how odd charisma should happen for one, and for no apparent reason such an affect just did not come along with another, no matter how much everyone loved or wished for it. Yet, the days, the years of living with all the experiences, including illnesses, celebrations, trials, and joys of marriage, children, parents, families and friends came to create an abundance of beauty and love and a belonging unmatched by any infatuation or magical scheme.

One did wonder about truth, not of spirit or of the soul, but of circumstance and what might be discovered after death about well-timed and well-meaning and well-cared for decisions. She made certain everyone knew beyond any question of their importance to her through her grand unconditional love.

Pain had climbed the walls then receded subsequent to her request for some relief. Death had lost its power, replaced with curiosity on the last phase of life. She smiled whimsically and humorously at the irony of perceptions interrupted, as she considered how: Being able to secure one's pathway to the restroom in some ways had become prerequisite for clarity of critical thinking regarding love.

My Heroes

I was born and abandoned in 1948 in Seoul, South Korea. I learned later, my mother implored my father to find an American adoption agency to secure her baby's (my) future. I ended up with a

Canadian husband and an American wife, informed their new baby had derived from brilliant parents and therefore would fit in well with them, two professors at the University of Toronto who desperately wanted me, since they could not have children of their own. Jacqueline Gunther lectured on art, including techniques, social influence, and history. Her work brought elegance and renown to the university's reputation. Leonard Gunther developed high-tech engineering programming to optimize communication systems. His work attracted innovative cutting-edge companies from all over the world, even Korea.

I read and spoke at an early age. Jacqueline and Leonard knew how to satisfy my curiosity, nourished by creative and logical processes involving thinking, living, experimenting, failing, succeeding, and just being. My childhood came with fun. They knew how to pique my interest and generate excitement as the three of us explored different rivers, harbors, lakes, glaciers, waterfalls, and countries, not to mention the simple things like rocks and mud, life, decay and petrification. Mom, who was from Santa Cruz, even taught me how to body surf when we went to California to visit her parents at Beer Can Beach. I had lots of questions, and they had lots of answers. The first time somebody at school called me something nasty because of the way I looked, I remember Mom told me, "The person who said that is an ignorant individual, unsophisticated and insecure. Who knows what has caused him to act like a bully? Even though bullies generally claim reasons for their behaviors, the rest of us have no obligation to endure their harmful behavior. Some people have said bad things to me because I am a woman and they don't think a woman has a right to the position I hold at the university. Some have said bad things to your father, because he is German, and they don't think anyone with German heritage should have a right to work in sensitive areas with computers."

As I listened to all her explanations, I kept wondering what in particular had people noticed about me, and I asked her.

"You, my love," she responded. "They can see you are half Korean."

"Where did I get that from?" I remember asking.

"From your father, who I have been told, was brilliant."

"But not from Dad..."

"No, not from Dad. Dad and I could not have babies, so we searched for you. You were given to us from the time you were born. That is how we became your mom and dad."

"Gerry says babies come out of their mothers. He said that was what happened to his sister."

"That's true."

"Did I come out of you?"

Mom shook her head slowly. "I am unable to bare children. So I prayed for us to meet you and your dad prayed for us to meet you, and we searched for you until you came to us."

Confusing, at five and a half, just starting school, these new ideas combined with other worries about just starting school. "Why?"

"Because you needed a mother and father, and we needed a baby. So we joined forces and became a family." Mom could tell I was confused. She looked worried, as if concerned about how I felt. How unlike her. I had never seen her worry about how I might react to what she had said. She pulled me to her and hugged me tight. She rocked me back and forth. "I love you so much, Ross. You are the best thing that ever happened to Dad and me. You fill our lives with love, and we have filled your life with love. Don't you think?"

I did think so. "Yes," I said. This became only the first of many conversations with Jacqueline or Leonard or both about the fact I was adopted. To make sure I had an idea of a culture representing someone who looked like me, Mom and Dad made sure I studied Korean history and familiarized myself with the Korean traditions, even as we continued to live in Toronto.

In 1967, after high school, I attended the University of Toronto, majoring in music, minoring in business during the day. At night, especially on Thursdays and Fridays, I loved playing Korean music in a small restaurant at dinnertime. In addition, quite often, I sat in with the Toronto rock band called Worthington Open or just The Open. I knew Jack Magee the guy who started the band, and he would let me play the keyboard. They had a gentle, lyrical sound. As a favor I introduced them to some people I knew at the University of Toronto who gave them more work.

One day the air spun with whirling secrets. Our family received an odd invitation to a concert sponsored by the Korean Consulate. In addition, The Worthington Open band had been invited to perform, but only if they added me to the group to play keyboard.

I met with Mom and Dad, and we concluded it must be some sort of joke. When I spoke with Jack Magee, he said, no joke. They told him some big wig in the consulate knew me. He suggested that was the primary reason The Open got the gig.

Dad called the Korean Consulate to inquire, for what purpose would we be receiving this sort of invitation. The Consulate assured Dad of the seriousness of the invitation, and they invited Mom and Dad to have lunch to discuss it.

The Consulate had scheduled the concert at the beginning of a two-week university break. Already, I had sat in with The Open on numerous occasions, learning a bit about how it might feel to be an actual professional musician. My parents had told me how proud I made them for excelling in classes and at the same time experimenting with music, which made me happy. But upon their return from the consulate, Jacqueline and Leonard acted peculiar.

I asked them, "What's going on?"

They shared a look with each other, then Dad started. "So, Ross, if you had to write a story about a guy who suddenly finds out surprising family information he never knew about, how would you construct it so it would have a successful uplifting denouement?"

I looked at him as if he had lost his mind. "Are you all right, Dad?"

"Well, yeah," he said. "I think so."

I turned to Mom, "Is Dad all right, Mom?"

She smiled mischievously. "When has your father ever been all right?"

We all laughed.

"Good point, Mom."

Mom faced Dad, "I don't think you've clarified the conditional circumstances that set up your story, Lenny."

"How am I supposed to do that?" asked Dad.

"Well, suppose someone who had a loving relationship with his parents but had no idea of the identity of his real father, but he would find out with a big surprise who is father was, can you envision the best way for that to happen..." She lifted her hands to emphasize the clarity of her suggestion.

With mom's clarity, came various realizations. Clearly, they had learned something about my biological father. I looked from one to the other. "Huh, hello."

Dad nodded his head slowly, "Yah. Hello."

Mom just simply said, "Hello, mellow, yellow." We all laughed again.

"Okay, what are you two up to?" I asked. "What have you learned or what do you know?"

Mom waved a hand, as if to let dad know she would take this one. "Sometimes things are strange. Sometimes they are strange and fascinating. Sometimes they are strange and scary. Sometimes they seem like they might have to be scary, but they really don't have to be."

I nodded, looked at Dad, and I looked askance back at Mom to let her know I was waiting for more.

I don't want to go further at this stage of my telling into what was said that night, because it would just be fair to say, Mom and Dad were the best two parents in the world to prepare me for the evening and the part I might play as a member of the band and as the biological son of someone famous who wanted to meet me.

The Korean Embassy had a ballroom and a theater beyond the dining hall. I recognized the food, every tasty morsel prepared by a combination of the Korean restaurants in the town. Afterwards, the joy I felt playing on the stage and watching Mom and Dad dance to our music thrilled me. When the party moved to the theater for a special presentation, the time came to present a Life Freedom Award by the Canadian government. The man, a Korean General, perhaps the most consequential in the history of South Korea, represented the pinnacle of achievement and courage. He entered the stage after being introduced by the Canadian Ambassador to Korea who enumerated a number of battles, policies, strategies made by this man. The man stood shorter than the ambassador, but his grand stature gave him command of the stage. Graciously, he accepted the honor. With every eye in the room riveted to him, he spoke eloquently of families, war, relationships, and gratitude to all his family and friends, and he particularly wanted to thank Jacqueline and Leonard Gunther, who he had never met until two days past, and their accomplished, brave, intelligent son, Ross, also one of his sons who he had never before met. A hush came over the audience. Then he called the three of us up to the stage to a substantial round of applause. The last moments of the evening ended with weird conversations, awkward questions, and enlightened facts well beyond my assimilation. This Korean General, now the Korean Ambassador to Canada, had been researching information about me and Jacqueline and Leonard for a couple of years.

The event came to an end, and I had to use the restroom. Mom and Dad continued outside. As I departed to join my parents, I was stopped by a Canadian official, who touched my arm and spoke, "I am a member of the Canadian International Service. I wanted to let you know, his excellency invites you to visit Korea and remain with him and all members of his family, any time and for as long as you wish at your desire."

I nodded politely and extended my hand. He took it, and we shook without me uttering a word, for I had nothing to say.

As I descended the steps, I thought of that little peninsula, always in jeopardy between China, Russia, and now North Korea, such bravery, always fighting for survival. I had pride as a Korean. Yet, as I found Mom and Dad waiting for me at the foot of the stairs, my overwhelming disposition cried out with joy and love. They were my heroes, not some famous man who the world thought was greater than so many others and so worthy of celebratory acclaim who so many people had endorsed as great and who had never during all those years wanted anything to do with me.

Martha

The hot evening summer air whooshed about KN's head. Stinging bits of sand, like buckshot, flipped into his face. Repeatedly, he blinked his eyes and looked left, toward the back of the train. The greed of the spinning steel, their heavy load clickety-clacketing atop the fitted rails, yawned as it patiently awaited him. In the darkness of the freight car's underbelly, KN saw his friend Phil, a little younger, also thirteen, a few feet away. Just the top of his head showed, hair wildly fanning in the rush, his shadow frozen like a spider. Phil had tied a bandana around his ears coat-collar-tight. KN had not seen him move since Sioux City. What did it take to remain so immobile? KN squirmed on his board positioned across the rods. His knees ached. His right foot had fallen asleep. He kicked above him against one of the floor joists, causing a corner of the board to slip off the rods. Instantly, an electrical impulse shot KN's arms whirling around the rod and from the underneath he slapped the board back into place. Sudden slipping and jerking jolted him with fear and he willed himself to turn his body slowly, as his heart thumped in his chest. KN envisioned himself as a sloth, slow moving and under control continually pursuing safe realignment of his balance. He wondered what sloths contemplated to keep their focus. For KN, focus revolved around Martha, conjuring feelings of warmth, windows of joy, her creamy white skin, smooth to the touch, her voice friendly and welcoming, her hands soft, but not as soft as her lips when she pressed them to his. She obscured the fear of tumbling along the planks with the whirling wheels of the train.

The way her face glowed when he asked her to the hayride, she seemed so excited. It had taken so long for him to ask. He had never been with a girl on a date. He could not imagine why she would want to be with him. Nor did he understand why he so wanted to be with her. He had seen her show great kindness to a brain-injured kid in their school, helping him one time when he fell, so much so, he joined her and they both walked him to the nurse. Even so, relief overwhelmed him when after hearing him ask, she did not even hesitate to say yes. Her eyes softened and rested on his. Her cheeks flushed with pink, more than usual. She seemed to come alive in a different way than he had previously observed. A wave of curiosity grew within him to discover more about the new aspects of Martha. He found himself observing her more closely. She became more than the kindest person he knew and the second fastest runner in the school who had once beat him in a race, or one of the best baseball players in the school who could hit the ball better than ninety percent of the boys, or the best horseback rider of any age who nobody came close to beating at the state fair. He learned Martha could hold her own with anybody. He learned having her on his team always increased the odds of winning. He learned paying particular attention to the questions she answered in school meant you would learn something not just new, but also unexpected and interesting. He had admired her even more after her father abandoned the family. During this hardship, he spent a lot of time with her, talking, listening, and supporting her daily battles to overcome heartbreak. However, the night of the hayride opened KN's awareness of Martha beyond his expectations and imagination.

Martha wanted a soda so they departed the dancehall

outside to the grass at the edge of the fields. Alone at the re-
freshment stand, Martha giggled and took his hand and
pulled him along a path away from the hoe-down and into
a clump of trees.

He remembered how it shocked him. "What're you
doing, Martha?"

"Shhh," she said.

She sounded like she had planned something. He could
hear every crackle of twigs, as she led him deeper into the
shadows. It seemed the noise of the twigs and the brush
scratching his jeans and then of Martha's voice whispering
words all made such a ruckus, surely everyone at the hoe-
down would have been able to hear and by now he figured
all knew where they were, away from everyone else and
alone. KN strained to see through the darkness, then he noticed Martha studying him intently.

"Karl Newton, whatever are you doing?" She liked challenging him, and she had a lilt in her tone as if about to laugh.

Confounded and curious, words did not form an idea.
"Nothing."

"It doesn't look like you're doing nothing."

"I'm just listening."

Martha giggled and squeezed both his hands. "Nobody's
followed us."

"I wouldn't care if they had..." Even as he said it, KN
knew she could tell a lie when she heard it.

She laughed quietly. "You look so serious."

"Don't mean to."

She stuck her face closer to his. "I'm having fun, KN. I
like teasing you."

KN listened to the voices and the music of other people.
"I feel a little weird, Martha."

"Why?"

"About being alone with you at night here in secret."

"K.N., do you like being alone with me?"

Thrilling, hard for him to describe it to himself any other way, "Yeah, uh-huh, I sure do."

She took both his hands in hers and lifted them level with her shoulders. "Then why do you feel weird?"

"Martha, I don't know." For some reason he raised her left hand to his lips and kissed her knuckles. He watched her turn her head toward him. A peacefulness overcame him and he smiled, relieved to talk it out. "I guess it's somethin' we've never done before."

She rolled their hands over and kissed his knuckles. His calming continued and transitioned to something new, a passion with acceptance going somewhere. Their sounds did not seem so loud among the natural melodies of the crickets, frogs, fiddler's music, hand slapping and distant laughter of the folk dancers.

Martha's whispered wistfully, "Would you like to kiss me?"

Curious, beyond belief, he could not fathom she would really want to kiss him. "On the hand again?"

She smiled, "No, not on the hand, KN."

He had wondered how exactly to go about it. "I've never kissed a girl before."

"I'd like to teach you." She turned her head away for a moment. "If I didn't think you were a kind, smart person and somebody I really liked and someday thought I might be able to love, because I do not want to end up like my parents, I would not be having fun with you like this."

He had not previously thought about many of those ideas and had no clue how to respond. "Okay."

"How do you feel about me?" she asked.

"I really like you, Martha. I think you're the kindest and smartest person in the entire school."

"And you know what? I think the same about you." She smiled and moved her face closer to him. "Go like this and we'll touch lips."

He did. Her soft warm puckered lips sent him reeling with new sensations. His heart leapt halfway up his throat. Her lips moved or quivered. He wondered what she was doing and how she was doing it. It had such an effect. His pulse throbbed as Martha pulled her head away.

She studied him. "How did you like it?"

KN took a deep breath. "Wow!" His breathing continued heavily. "I never knew that's what happens with a kiss!"

Martha laughed, she too, a little breathless. "Yes, I know what you mean."

"You wanna do it again?" asked KN. When she hesitated, he added, "I just wanna see if what I felt could happen again."

Martha gave him a funny look. "I think you already know the answer to that one, and if I'm honest, so do I."

This time Martha tilted her head slightly back and closed her eyes. KN bent down and touched his lips to hers. He then let his arms encircle her waist and her back. Firmly, he held her close, so their bellies and their hips and their torsos touched. For KN, Martha had lifted him to a level of new, spectacular sensations. It took him a moment to realize Martha's hands pushed firmly against his chest.

He stopped the kiss and released her. He tried to catch his breath, and she hers.

He held her shoulders. "Are you all right? Did I do something wrong?"

Martha still had one hand on him, as if she wanted to

continue touching him, but she had to ward him off. "No. You're doing great. Too great, KN. Are you sure you never kissed a girl before?"

"Martha, you are the first."

"Whew," sighed Martha. "I'm afraid to kiss you any more right now. That was quite something."

They always ended their kissing with Martha making similar comments. He smiled to himself. For a long while he had not tracked her meaning. Martha, such a great friend, he truly loved her and never tired of thinking of her.

Splash went the wind. The roaring clickety-clacks cracked their pattern at a furious pace, as the train rocked back and forth. The track bed painted a dizzy brown blur. KN tightened his grip on the rod and tried to stabilize his board. It kept shifting with the hurtling machine. As a passenger he had never realized the conditions below the under part of the train, the iron, timbers of wood, and steel tied together forming one engineering marvel always willing to squish the flesh, muscle and bone of a thirteen-year-old kid who wanted to see fourteen. Fatigue and continuing to fight off sleep meant he would survive another hour. Jaw set and aching, knuckles tight and squeezed white, the train roared into a tunnel and he could no longer see his hands, just like he could no longer see Phil, even though he thought he knew Phil's exact location. But he thought he heard a scream. He could not be sure comparing screams with the screeching of the welcoming wheels. Just hanging on now, the dark had turned pitch black.

KN yelled as loud as he could, "Phil're you okay?!" Even if as he hollered with the calamitous cries of the engine ricocheting off the tunnel walls, he wondered if any sound he made could have been heard by Phil. KN knew any movement, such as inching his way over the rods to where he had last seen Phil on his board, might jeopardize the precarious balance of either. They had decided to ride the rods and swing into position together, but now in the jumpy darkness of the train's underbelly each had responsibility for themselves to hang on and survive. As the locomotive hurled them beyond the tunnel, even then, the shadows had sustained the strain of sightlessness. KN knew his responsibility meant keeping hope and positive ideas in his head, so he had continued his reminiscences of Martha.

Fifteen years later, now 1919, he had renewed contacts in Michigan, visiting his family home, occupied by his oldest brother. To everyone's amusement, he and Phil, who had moved back to the old neighborhood, entertained the Michiganders with stories about those adventurous times back as a kids on the rods. KN had the most to tell, as he had worked in San Francisco, Seattle, Los Angeles, and more recently the Monterey Peninsula. He had seen things people in his hometown had not experienced, but they knew more about local news, the whole state agog over Martha's success in film and silent movies. Once he returned home to San Francisco, he discovered her entourage had brought her to the Central Coast. He packed his bags, hopped aboard a train southbound to connect with the Del Monte Express he had ridden many times with friends, companions, and clients. One developed roads through the Del Monte Forest. Another owned the Highlands Inn, renovated so successfully in 1917 and located three miles south of the artists' village of Carmel, also in continual development. New resorts needed friendly systems in place to set up races, polo matches, cricket games, community halls, swimming pools, tennis courts, hiking adventures, art displays and classes for art, golf, biking, horseback riding, or surfing. On one occasion KN had flown in to the Del Monte Airport with Samuel F B Morse, the manager of the Pacific Improvement Companies and the new owner of the entire Del Monte Forest, on his way to meet J. F. Devendorf, the Carmel area's main owner and developer, who hired him to run activities and promotions to ensure ever-growing numbers of happy visitors and guaranteed fiscal successes. Good fortune allowed KN to work for both men, each considered among the most influential and far-sighted developers of the Peninsula during those years.

KN always booked a seat on the righthand side of the train, as hints of coastal panoramas rather than mountain views gave him the greatest pleasure and peace. The luxury car glided west, south of the City of Watsonville and into Castroville through large fields covered with deep red dots of strawberries and then artichokes as far as one could see. He could taste the sweetness of the strawberries and the green meat of the artichokes cooked just right and covered in butter. In a way he envied the farmers with houses sitting on knolls surrounded by sweet crops with an even sweeter western view of the Pacific Ocean. As he rode above the Elkhorn Slough, he almost always saw egrets, pelicans, hawks, deer, and elk. Distant paddling kayakers seemed enthralled with Nature's surrounding splendor. The Salinas river, particularly vibrant in the spring and early summer, lay against roads heading back toward Salinas. The tracks paralleled Highway 1 spanning their own river bridges south to Marina, Fort Ord, Seaside, Monterey, Pebble Beach, or Pacific Grove. Of course, most people disembarked at the Del Monte Hotel, the most elegant establishment of its kind on the entire west coast. However, KN had a different destination.

He changed to the freight train. It allowed him to check various projects he had worked on for Samuel Morse, improving the racetrack, modifying the polo field, bringing horse trails and walking paths up to standard. He stepped off at Spanish Bay. Happily, he noticed the morning fog had lifted, leaving dry riding trails and roads to Carmel, along the 17 Mile Drive, if he chose. He knew a woman who owned a ranch near the water. Often he spent time with her. On many occasions they had ridden two of her American Saddlebreds through the Del Monte Forest where they could find their own hidden spot surrounded with old growth cypress trees or cedar coves or lines of Monterey pines overlooking whitewash waves or groups of sailing vessels. Sometimes they watched polo matches or road races. Today, however, she knew he would be riding alone into Carmel.

From the cliffs just beyond the new Del Monte Lodge, the new golf course, finished earlier that year in February, had closed pathways near the ocean. Even so, the views of Point Lobos and the sight of the Carmel Bay through and over the pines created great anticipation. He tied off the reigns on the street below the Pine Inn, the most celebrated hotel in the village.

Once inside, he found the manager, also an acquaintance, who guided KN to where he needed to be.

Now he stood across the restaurant from an alluring blond woman the same age as he. She had not seen him. She had her head tilted slightly with a man pressing his lips against her cheek. KN pondered what they were to each other. He waited until their laughter had subsided and the two had settled across from each other before he sauntered over the polished wooden floors to their table on a small balcony just outside and overlooking the ocean.

When the woman noticed him, she seemed curious. The man not so much. KN spoke before the man could make an inquiry.

"It's been a long time since the hay-ride, Martha. Just thought I'd stop and say hello."

Martha's eyes widened with delight. "KN!" She jumped up and threw her arms around him.

"Who the hell is this?" asked the man.

"This is my childhood chum, KN!"

KN gasped at the effects of the hug. Martha still knew how to press against him.

"This isn't any practice scene for an upcoming movie, George, this is real life, an old-time friendship." Martha took KN's hand and pulled him away from the table and inside the restaurant.

"We had a date," said George.

Martha looked back over her shoulder, "You were asking me for a donation to your charity, George. There will be other times to work together." As they walked away, she whispered to KN, "But not today!"

KN's chest throbbed as it had so many years before. He had never met another woman who came close to causing him to feel the way he used to feel around Martha. "Where're we headin'?"

Martha's lips twisted in a mischievous grin. "Somewhere to catch up. You ever thought about me?"

He smirked. "Every minute of every day."

She laughed. "I know that isn't true!" As they crossed the restaurant, she pulled on his coat and he pretended she had enough force to draw him to her.

His head landed close to her ear. "I've thought about you more than you know."

She pushed him away to see his eyes. He knew she could tell he meant it. "Okay," she said. "Well, I've thought about you too."

She danced down the carpeted stairway along the wooden sidewalk and across Ocean Avenue and he followed.

"This is my car." She placed her hand on a Model T. She leaned back as if posing for a photo.

KN took in a deep breath and exhaled. "All right." She made herself look captivating, like the movie star everybody knew, especially in front of artists' studios displaying colorful decor, paintings, and other works of art in the storefronts along the street behind her. Not too many women had their own automobile in this or any other town. And none others had such charisma.

"Want to give a crank?"

"Sure."

KN took the metal handle in front of the radiator and waited for Martha to get seated in the car. It looked brand new. When she signaled, he pushed and the engine started with only a partial flip.

KN hopped into the passenger seat and nodded appreciatively. "Pretty spiffy."

Martha smiled and pushed the low gear pedal. "I'm glad you like it. Because I'm going to be taking you for a ride."

They exchanged a look and they both laughed, as he reflected once again about all those times over the years he had lost himself in thought, reflecting about kind-hearted Martha, the smartest person he had ever met.

On the Way to Desperation

For weeks, like a windblown vessel, Jesse drifted along sidewalks and earthen paths through suburbs, forests, cities, country streets, and towns, but tonight, in the middle of winter, fatigue having smashed his keen awareness of danger and of positioning through a myriad of topographical environs, he really had no idea of his location nor of the immediate conditions which had enveloped him. Even though a number of people in the foster care system thought him too stupid or lacking curiosity for school, he knew his functioning had nothing to do with school. He had lost interest in participating with other humans. For him living meant existence *without hope*.

"How old are you, kid?"

Jesse had not actually heard the words. He had heard vague sounds, like gurgling. It took his mind a while to calculate any meaning. Painful recollections and their residues had pushed out the awareness of being. Inundated with obstructionist daydreams of obscure and distorted relationships promoting vague representations of *knowns* and *unknowns*, while contemplating the mystery behind the relevance of what had taken hold of him, he had become lost in unquestioned clarity of some things and utter confusion of others. Perhaps by instinct, perhaps by chance, he had stopped his drifting long enough on this freezing, harsh, windblown evening to discover himself standing, a complete surprise to him, with a group of people in a makeshift line near the exterior of a homeless shelter, just up from the shoreline of the eastern side of the San Francisco Bay.

He turned to decry a dirty, disheveled, run-down, middle-aged white man apparently studying him. "Wh-what?"

"I said, *How old are you?*"

The man smelled like a seaweed sea. Jesse said nothing. He turned and met the man's gaze.

"I bet you ain't more than twelve or thirteen."

The man had wrapped himself in damp blankets and plastic with crusty splotches, perhaps salt. Jesse imagined the man bathing in the sea, as if to create a new coat. He realized the peculiarity of this thought, but then so many of his perceptions had become so peculiar.

"Where are you from?"

Jesse caught a waft of bourbon, recently consumed. He surmised the man had booze in one of the protective folds of his garment. He tried to ignore the drunk without success, as the man repeatedly tapped on his shoulder. Finally, he turned.

Now he faced watery red eyes attempting to appear penetrating, friendly, and alert, as if to project a portrait of empathy. Jesse wondered if the man were dangerous, psychotic, perverted, or just disengaged by happenstance, such as enduring wrongful actions designed yet failing to establish late in life successes.

"None of your business."

"Just curious."

The drunk's demeanor transformed from one pre-occupied with self to one suddenly animated and pointing his index finger towards Jesse.

"You need to ask for help."

How odd, a drunken white guy in his forties, standing in a line outside a homeless shelter, offering him advice. In truth, Jesse had asked for help from innumerable sources with perennial empty responses, causing him to uncover and understand the resolute depth beneath disappointment and helplessness.

The man waited until Jesse faced him once again. "You need to pray to God our Father and to Jesus Christ." He fully extended his thickly covered arm upward and he stared at the overcast sky. The man's face seemed changed in the light. Jesse wondered if he were partly Egyptian or Indian or even Asian. Jesse concluded the man might be Native American. Like a living kaleidoscopic apparition, in Jesse's mind, he transformed through universal personages.

The older voice trembled through the words, "God is the only one who will listen!" The man's forehead became more deeply lined as he scowled and his attention waned. Just as suddenly lines softened. The man turned into himself and muttered, "God is the only entity who can actually do anything to help."

For a moment, the splashing of the bay and the distant barking of sea lions caught Jesse's attention. He scanned the darkly lit buildings blocking his view of the waterfront.

The man thrust his face forward, stepping toward Jesse. "Who is your God?" The man's hand disappeared into the warmth of his cocoon and returned with a pint of Jim Beam. He offered it to Jesse.

"No thanks," said Jesse.

The man took a long swig and did not return the bottle to its hiding place. "They won't let me bring it with me, so…"

Jesse wondered what luck this man had with prayer, or whether the man believed himself better off since the last time he prayed. If so, Jesse supposed, previously, the man must have existed in even more horrendous conditions.

Jesse waited so as to have the right demeanor before he let go of the words, without sarcasm, just a desire for information on what made prayer so great the man would implore others to do it. "What have you gained from prayer?"

The man's mood lightened immediately and to Jesse's surprise, he laughed. His laugh brought a transition free of trouble and full of joy. "That's a good question." He raised his bottle to the night. "I have gained much from prayer!"

"Like what?" Jesse wanted to hear, because he had done a lot of praying in that Christian foster home and had gained nothing from it. As an afterthought he added, "And why were you laughing?"

The man smiled and he took another swig of bourbon. "I laughed because of the irony."

Once again, the man's accent confounded Jesse, and he wondered about his heredity, his education, and where he was from.

"And I enjoy your understanding of the irony how one who claims to have prayed to the Almighty is in such a state, as I am in...." A knowing smile settled on the man's face. "I appreciate your kindness in the way you asked me about it, with such sincerity, so I believe it is a question you are truly contemplating, such as, 'why isn't the Lord helping me' meaning you more than I!"

The man studied Jesse, as if to verify what he had just stated. "You really do need to talk to God. I think he really will listen to someone like you." When he saw Jesse analyzing him in the same way as he had been analyzing Jesse, the man lifted the pint and offered it to Jesse again. When again Jesse declined, the man drained the rest of the bottle.

The drunk's eyes brightened, as if in some way observing the personification of magnificence. "Every day I used to get down on my knees and pray. And every day God answered my prayers."

Impressed by the man's apparent transitions, Jesse simply uttered, "How do you know he was answering your prayers?"

"By giving me opportunities, lots of them. Lots more than I ever had before. Opportunities I never would have had without God's help, at least this is my perception."

Jesse shook his head. "What about now?"

"I don't want His help now, so much. I don't deserve it. I deserve to be free of all connections."

"I thought you didn't have to earn God's love."

"So they say. A sometimes Truth!"

"You say you deserve to be free, but you don't seem very free," said Jesse

"I am separated. Separation is a form of freedom." Then in a whisper, the drunk added, "Anyway, I am unwilling to repent."

Jesse doubted such an admission would come from a pervert or a molester. Still, he had a general mistrust of all adults and drunkards and addicts in particular. Yet, the drunk had triggered some memories and they were the type of memories always returning to haunt Jesse. He considered the futility of yet another discussion on the subject, but then decided why not determine if this man had a new or relevant perspective.

The drunk seemed to realize Jesse was about to say something important. He widened his eyes and turned his head directly toward Jesse.

"I have prayed to God," said Jesse. "I prayed to God every day, several, no, many times every day and at first it helped me. It helped me because I thought God was going to do something. I thought he would do something to make the pain go away and to make my life and my mother's life better, so we could survive and have some peace, a peaceful heart and some hope..."

"And?"

"And then..." said Jesse, " He did nothing."

Jesse could almost taste the numbness in his voice, dry and soft, matter of fact, as if describing an old idea rattling through his mind for so long he had gone through anger and disappointment and other stages, evolving all the way to acquiescence of such a tragic realization.

The drunk waited. Perhaps too drunk to quickly respond, he appeared deep in reflection, as Jesse settled in with the circumstances he had described.

"You prayed and prayed and He did nothing," said the drunk.

"That's' right," said Jesse.

The door to the shelter opened and the line along the sidewalk became animated. The homeless mass pushed them toward the entrance.

After a few moments and they had walked a few steps, Jesse felt a hand on his shoulder. He suddenly feared he had misjudged the old drunk. In alarm he hurled himself backwards and turned to face the man. Once again the old face surprised Jesse. For an instant the drunk's eyes seemed clear, almost alert, as if they belonged to a highly paid advisor to the President of the United States or something.

"They won't let you in by yourself," he said.

"Why not?"

"You're too young. You need to be my son, just pretend."

"What if I don't want to?"

"You'll do something else, go somewhere else. I don't know."

Jesse kept his eye on the man at the door, inspecting then letting some people in.

"God will do something...in His own time," said the drunk.

"I've heard that before," said Jesse.

The drunk nodded and waited for Jesse to go ahead of him. Now with the drunk in line behind him, Jesse heard him continue to mutter, "It's always in His own time..."

Jesse passed through the door. The warmth of the shelter summoned him. "Just a moment, son. You got a parent?"

The black man at the door looked past him, "You! You're drunk! Again!"

From behind him he heard the drunk plead, "I'm not that drunk!"

"You wait outside and maybe sober up a little. We don't want no trouble tonight!"

"It's cold out here."

Jesse turned to face the doorman. "I don't want to be in here without my father."

"Your father? I've never seen you before, and I see him all the time! And..." The doorman glanced from one to the other, "You two look nothing alike!"

"My mother's homeless too," said Jesse. "And she gave up on me."

The doorman looked at Jesse and once again back at the drunk. Jesse followed his gaze. For a moment the drunk seemed darker, as if he had become Hispanic or even black followed by a sudden transformation to very pale. Jesse wondered how the light might have created such an appearance, as if they really could have been related. Suddenly, the doorman pulled the drunk just inside and he squeezed him against the wall. "Okay, we'll make an exception for your kid, but as for you? We'll see how much you sober up; maybe we'll let you stay. If not, you can meet up with your kid in the morning."

By the time Jesse arose in the morning to get breakfast, the drunk was gone. Jesse discovered the doorman had allowed *his father* to spend the night inside.

"I wouldn't have done it if you hadn't put in a good word for him." He continued refilling people's coffee mugs. "And he knew it, too. I've thrown him out many a' time. I like helpin', but I don't want no trouble. But it surprises me he just left you here. Alone."

"Or that he was even able to get up so early," said Jesse.

"You mean how far gone he was... It is surprising sometimes, how he always sobers up so fast."

Jesse had eaten enough pancakes to fill him up for the first time in days.

When the man saw Jesse gathering his bag as if to leave, he set the coffee pot on the table and faced Jesse. "Now, you ain't really that drunk man's boy, are you?"

The question caught Jesse off guard and he found himself thinking about what he should say.

"How old are you, son?"

"Sixteen."

"You ain't no sixteen. You're about twelve, fourteen at the outside."

"I'm sixteen, Sir."

What's your name?"

"Somebody Somebody."

The man laughed. "Well, Somebody Somebody, where do you live?"

"What's your name?" asked Jesse.

"Trenton. Around here they call me Mr. T."

"What's your name? Where're you from? Why aren't you in school? How many foster homes've you been in? How many more do you want to be in? And by law, you, as manager of this care center, have to call Child Protective Services when a boy my age shows up, right?"

"That's right. I have called them already. Once I saw your *dad* take off."

"Well, I know the routine. How long will it take them to get here?"

"I don't know. They're busy. I know I can't just let you leave. You have to wait until they get here."

"Okay," said Jesse. "I might as well have another orange juice."

"Might as well," said Mr. T.

The room still crowded with folks eating and lounging on their cots, before long Jesse had lost track of Mr. T. Perhaps he had returned to the kitchen for more coffee or maybe other people standing around had blocked the sight of him. Whatever the situation, Jesse needed to use the restroom, whether CPS was on the way or not.

Once he finished washing his hands, he opened the bathroom window, tossed his bag into the alley, and followed after it. He closed the window from the outside, and as he turned to face the day, he caught a glimpse of a man sitting on a crate and watching him. It was the drunk, now apparently sober and appearing very Asian.

"Did you have a nice breakfast?"

"Are you a cop?"

"Me?"

"A private investigator?"

"No..."

"A pervert."

"No, way."

"You're mighty awake for somebody who was so drunk last night."

"I have a quick recovery rate."

"Well," said Jesse, "I'd like to stay here and chat, but I've got to keep movin'."

"Yeah. Pretty soon they'll realize you've escaped."

"That's right."

As Jesse walked quickly down the alley, the man fell in step. "Who are you anyway?" asked Jesse. "And where are you from? Every time I take a look at you, you seem to be different. Are you white? Asian? African? Indian? Mexican? A combination…?"

The man looked askance. "It's not polite to ask."

"Sometimes you seem black…" Jesse took a closer look.

The man changed again.

"Or even Hispanic, like now, whiter and more Hispanic than Asian or black."

The man shrugged. "I'd like to help you."

"Normally, I would have concluded you are a pervert, but the way my perceptions of you keep changing, I'm not sure what's going on."

"I want to repay a favor."

"I did you no favor."

"You got me shelter and a meal."

"I made one comment."

"Sometimes that's all it takes."

"And it was you who enabled me to get in," said Jesse.

"We helped each other. Of course, without you…Once they kick you out, they never let you back in."

Jesse shook his head at how alert the man seemed. "I can't believe how fast you sobered up."

"I'm the same as I was last night. And now, just like then, I recognize you."

"You don't recognize me."

"I recognized you from somewhere."

"Bullshit."

"From memories."

"We don't share any memories…"

"Memories of those I have known…"

"Like memories you're making up as you go along."

Jesse sped up as they approached the end of the alley, and the man grabbed his arm.

"I can help you."

His face, now brown, seemed intelligent and wise, friendly and determined. "Here." He handed Jesse several twenty-dollar bills. "Call me, if you become desperate. My number's in there. Or just keep the cash, if that's all you need. I know a place you can stay sometime."

Jesse handed the cash back to him. "It's as if you are perverted…"

"I am not perverted." The man picked his card out of the cash and stuck it into Jesse's pocket. "I mean it. If you need help or a place to stay, call that number."

On one hand, Jesse figured he would encounter a number 10-magnitude earthquake with San Francisco skyscrapers collapsing into the lower city beneath the real city before he called that drunk or entered his domain. On the other hand, he wondered if there was a chance the man, given all his imperfections, was just trying to do good and instill hope in others, especially those, like Jesse, on the road to desperation. Jesse was feeling more positive.

After substantially increasing his distance from the homeless shelter, Jesse turned to see what the man was doing now. At first glance, Jesse did not see him, so he stopped.

His eyes searched in every direction.

To his surprise the man was gone.

Against The Current

Kit entered the penthouse and placed his jacket over a hook on the inside of the entry closet door. He poured Laurel's filtered water into a Heisey tumbler. He walked to the wall of windows overlooking San Francisco Bay. From there he caught a glimpse of the Golden Gate estuary and Richardson Bay. One could view Ferries crossing to Sausalito from the outside garden balcony. Throughout their marriage they had lived in London, New York and Paris, but San Francisco embraced his spirit more than the others. He turned in the direction of the main door. He set the water on a marble-topped table. He picked up the book he had read and prepared to discuss. He reclined in the adjacent Chesterfield high back winged chair. He wanted to observe the woman beloved even more than she knew from the moment she entered.

Laurel handed the cabbie five times more than usual and caught the eye of the friendly concierge.

"Hello, Mrs. Jones."

"Hello, Everett!"

"How are you today?"

"Good." She smiled and took in a long full breath.

As she strode across the lobby, she hoped Kit's tryst had been as successful for him as hers had for her.

The little man pulled the elevator open. "Hello, Mrs. Jones."

"Hello, Ted. How are you this cool, bright day?"

"It's had some ups and downs."

She smiled more than usual. "Again?"

"Just about all the time! I can count on it!"

The door opened with a swish. Kit stood and listened.

Heels clicked through the foyer. Her radiant appearance rounded the corner, an open coat flowing along with a compliment of festive clothing creating a dramatic, breathtaking visage, bubblier than a new year's celebration as if returning from an exhilarating quest. Kit's afternoon had gone well, still he felt a pang of envy. He surmised his dalliance had less impact on him than hers did have on her. He wanted to say something to conceal his pain. "You look new!"

Laurel thought to herself, *Who is that handsome gentleman before me? He has such dignity and integrity and understanding and pride. He would never show his pain.* "And you look grand, in some sense elevated."

"Oh, have you been talking to Ted?"

Laurel laughed. "Of course."

"Did you confide in him about our plan?"

Laurel feigned disbelief. "Why, no. There were far too many ups and downs discussed to consider any literary elucidations."

Kit swirled his glass of water. "I can tell you are ready to discuss the book."

"Yes. As we said we would. These are the times of some of our best discussions."

Kit picked up the novel. "This one, not as many people are reading, as I would have thought."

"I know. It's a shame, really, don't you think?"

"I do." Kit glanced at the cover. "F. Scott Fitzgerald, *The Great Gatsby*." He could see she looked forward to hearing his opinions. "Knowing him a little, not as much as you, I can see how he managed to orchestrate this time of glamour, corruption, and extravagance with shards of his own history."

Laurel nodded, "Yes." She saw, once again, Kit had a clear understanding of one of her books. "Do you mind?"

He watched her meander to the liquor cabinet and lift a bottle of bourbon from the shelf. "I would have thought you would have already..."

"Oh, no. Like when we spend our time with each other..."

Kit shrugged and smiled a little. "I thought you might have needed something..."

"To get in the mood?" asked Laurel.

"I guess not." Stressful pretending nothing different had happened today, his eyes followed her as she scurried to the refrigerator and dropped ice cubes from the freezer into her glass. She moved with such grace. "Daisy could be with Tom or Gatsby."

"Not necessarily in equal measure," said Laurel.

When she had returned to the sofa, Kit raised the Heisey tumbler. "Here's to another great afternoon for all!"

"To well-made and implemented plans!" She held her drink high.

As their eyes met, Kit appeared calm. He directed his facade to mirror peace, to smear and shield the pain with a glorious smile.

Laurel wanted to hide both her joy over the afternoon and the sadness she felt because of it. She knew these feelings would slide away, as these types of remembrances existed for finite durations, not like their relationship, hers and Kit's.

Eyes locked in enough for each to see how the conversation would continue.

"What do you think of the last line in the book?" asked Kit.

Laurel had it memorized. "And so we beat on, boats against the current, borne back ceaselessly into the past."

The ideas bore too tight an analogy for her to continue. Sometimes she hated to be first, especially when discussions were about to turn serious. Advising on the editing of this book brought so much so close. She turned in silence. Her eyes drifted to the view of the bay.

Kit downed the water in his glass and sauntered to where Laurel had left the fifth of bourbon. He thought about adding ice, then decided against it. "You see yourself as Daisy?"

"I'm definitely not Myrtle."

"Or Jordan Baker," he added. "And who am I, then? Am I in the story?"

"You are way too accomplished to be Nick and way to sophisticated to be Tom. You are too smart and debonaire to be Myrtle's husband."

"And as we beat on in this first quarter of the twentieth century, are we ceaselessly borne back into the past? And are the years and times, not only two peoples', but is everybody in this careless hour of 1925 unknowingly trapped in the boats against the current?"

Laurel lifted a pack of cigarettes from between her breasts and bounced it so three smokes stood above the rest. "I'm going to take a moment to break down the meaning of all you have just said."

Kit laughed and grabbed a lighter from his pocket.

"Do you want one?" asked Laurel.

"No thanks."

They took a few steps nearer the windows where they could see past Angle Island to the other side of the Bay. He lit her cigarette. Laurel inhaled deeply and blew the smoke so it would not drift against his face. "I'll never tire of this view."

"Me neither." He caught foreign scents emanating from her skin. He opened the door leading to the outer garden balcony. "It is rather cool outside," said Laurel.

Kit brought the door back, leaving a mere slice for air to flow. "Just a bit of fresh air."

"Maybe we should shower off."

Kit nodded. "Yes."

"You don't see yourself as Gatsby?" asked Laurel.

"There are parallels," said Kit. "He had to impress a wealthy socialite, and like the circular plot of a movie, he had to become something more than where he had begun, and I suppose even given the power of their love, the twisting free-wheeling ties of the culture, the times entwined their relationship and wouldn't allow it to hold. Is that how you see us?"

Laurel placed her cigarette in the metal lip of the ash tray and hurried to Kit. She grabbed his broad shoulders. "These times allow us to be free and we are, and I love you." She kissed him passionately on the lips. It did not compare to the thrill she had experienced earlier in the day, but her real self with their real love always carried the potential to crescendo to double forte in any beat of any measure of any day.

Kit returned her kiss, as one in love would do for the person he loved. He allowed her to hug him. When his hand flattened and pulled on the back of her waist, bringing her to him, it seemed like the boats were turning and beginning to run with the current. He wanted to lift her to him and carry her away, but that foreign scent.

Laurel backed up to look him in the eye. "Let's wash off the afternoon."

He noticed Laurel's cigarette had burned to ash and had begun to descend from the tray. "Hold on." He pushed past her. The cigarette had fallen to the table. He grabbed it and smashed out its fire then left it where it belonged. "Do you want another drink?"

Laurel did want another drink, but she wanted to reassure him more. "I don't need another drink."

"Neither do I," said Kit. "But I'd like a short one just the same."

"We can take them to our modernized bathroom."

"Or enjoy the view here."

"I don't want another drink," said Laurel.

"Okay," said Kit. He took his time handling the bottle of bourbon. He poured three or four shots.

Laurel lifted the coat from her shoulders and threw it over a chair. As he finished his first swig, she grabbed his hand and began leading him toward the double headed Crane tiled shower overlooking a stunning panorama of the City, Market Street, and the Warf. "I'll share that drink with you."

He lifted it out of her reach. "I'm not so sure about that."

Letting him see her concern, Laurel touched his lips with her fingertips.

Knowing the past, having it ceaselessly drag him back. He nipped her fingers with his teeth. "We'll see," he said. It had been awhile since he felt darkness harden on such a beautiful day.

Laurel sensed something dangerously out of balance. She had wanted to kid with him and bring him around. Instead, she wondered if they had reached a new stage, some transition, perhaps of style or culture, so many perennial experiments seemed to change every day. She stopped, took his free hand with both of hers and pushed herself against the wall. She hung on tightly and waited for his anger to subside enough to meet her gaze.

Jacarandas

Snapping twig.

Hit the ground hard. Bullet zipping past my ear. Scurrying to a stone wall. Listening. Camera at the ready. Surrounded by death. Slug. A round hitting a nearby tree. A figure, in the air, through a camera lens in the limbs of a different tree. Snap. Snap. Someone fires two rounds. Shush-shush, thud. I spot movement on the ground. Snap. Snap. A person behind me fires more rounds quieting the movement. I'm near a village, under fire, reporting on the war.

And then I'm not.

I realize just another vision, what I have seen in my mind, so often, only this time not just envisioned. I have knelt for protection in the arms of the forest across a small lake from Aliah's hometown.

I stand and swat leaves and debris from my personally chosen funeral covering, a kaftan Islamic thobe. Across the lake I see the grove of jacaranda trees that have exploded into radiant purple and violet hues. Such a cascade of color can only be admired by those with the lightness of spirit to reflect on such beauty. That was not me on this day. As I await the pole-pushed ferry to transport me to the other side of the lake below the purple, I see, the underlying weeping shadows and a glimpse of a few individuals sauntering toward the funeral site. I am reminded of the tiny strip of water on the edge of my hometown Seaside, California, Laguna del Rey, a place I hope will be a future destination.

"I have never been in a boat on a lake before," Aliah speaking at another time and place.

The accent Australian, the voice from jannah, a young Pakistani woman, lyrical, bright, full of hope without expectations, matter of fact, peaceful, like the reporter she was. She would have loved seeing the jacaranda. She stood thin, but to me, wiry and elegant. I knew how her outward appearance masked the physical and mental strength, the agility, *nonpareil*, and toughness. She had to be like steel to succeed from where she had come and to get through what I had seen her get through in war. In peaceful times where women were not acknowledged, to survive she dressed and fought like a man. I came to love her more than anyone I had ever met.

"I've never paddled a canoe with a woman who has never been on a lake before."

She stared in such a way, I had begun to think I was about to be played. "Oh, I haven't been in a boat, but I have swum in a lake before."

Again, she caught me off guard, and as I laughed, I nearly tipped us over while pushing away from shore. "And you could be swimming again, if I don't get my balance righted." She laughed gaily and with me.

We had a lot of laughs that day and forever after. She lived for laughter and she thought me hysterically funny. She had no concerns that first time on the lake. She told me later, if I capsized the canoe, she would have saved me, if for some reason I had been unable to swim. Later she happened to mention push rafts were not boats.

Matching our schedules was like throwing pollen in the air. We took leave from the war and spent a week in Sydney, where she had so many friends, Australians, Pakistanis,

Afghans. No family though. Her family had been against her culturalization of the rest of the world. They did not allow her to attend university. They had sent her, the eldest daughter, to Australia to look after small children younger than school age for one year and then return home prepared. Her desire to become an educated war correspondent caused her father to feel betrayed and disown her. Even so, she still held them, her father, her mother, and her remaining brother and sisters in great affection.

As the raft approached the shore, I stepped toward the docking area. The passengers departed and at the beckoning of the pilot, a large man with a woman, and I, three people with covered heads, handed him coins and walked aboard. The wooden floor, dryer than I had imagined, rode high above the water. The woman sat on the smooth shiny wooden bench that fenced two sides of the raft. The large man leaned protectively over her.

The pilot commanded something I did not understand, then pushed the raft toward the main body of the lake. Expertly, he used his push pole to keep us floating directly toward the dock near the jacarandas. As we travelled over the surface, the large man changed his position slightly so I would have no vision of the woman.

Once I had debarked the raft, I walked with purpose toward the prayer room in the mosque adjacent to the cemetery. I had carefully chosen a Kufi commonly worn in Pakistan, so all would know I was Muslim and not be alarmed that I was not of their culture. In the mosque no questions would be asked, but after the funeral, when I went to the home, I wanted people to have seen me, so all would be comfortable with my presence.

Into the home I brought a large tray of food and flowers.

I asked to speak with the patriarch, Aliah's father. He looked old and sad and kindhearted. He also looked strong, uncompromising and tough. I waited in line. I handed my tray of food to one of the women. Somebody took the flowers. I really did not know any Urdu, the official language. Aware Aliah's father did speak English, I could only hope for good fortune, as I had no idea how I would be received. But I wanted a chance to bridge the gap of love I felt wrongly existed between this man and his daughter.

"Father, this is Mohamed Kahn."

I bowed. "Mr. Bukhari, I am so sorry for your loss."

When he heard my accent, he became alerted. "You're an American."

"I am Muslim. I am an American. I come representing Aliah. I came of my own accord to express her sorrow at the loss of her brother. His death is a great loss to her. She grieves losing the brother she loved so much and the brother she knows you loved so much."

Mr. Bukhari staggered back. Several other men around him moved protectively in front of him. Two grabbed me by the arm. They jerked me around and I had no idea regarding my safety. They lifted me off the ground.

"Nahi!" came a call. I was lowered.

"You!" It was Mr. Bukhari. He pointed to a door. "In there!"

I walked to the door and lifted the latch. Other men started to follow. Mr. Bukhari raised his hand and gave a nod. The other men stepped aside. Mr. Bukhari followed me into a smaller room, a sort of library with beautiful artifacts adorning the shelves. In the middle, two ornate chairs highlighted either side of an uneven marble topped table, acting as a realistic battleground for large carved combative looking chess pieces.

"Sit."

I took the chair furthest from the door. He remained standing.

"Who are you?"

"I am the Muslim who is in love with and wants to marry your daughter Aliah. I have brought you money from Aliah and me to give to the family of Arham, the one filled with compassion, a small representation of the sorrow Aliah and I feel for your loss. "

I placed the envelope containing the money on the chess table.

"My desire is to help heal the wounds between people who love each other. In the future, I would like to meet with you and ask you for Aliah's hand in marriage."

A tear fell from the lid of Mr. Bukhari's left eye. His head began shaking slightly. He took a deep breath. He pointed to a door on the far side of the room. He spoke quietly, "Go."

I stood uncertainly.

He thrust his finger toward the door, and the words hissed through his teeth. "Go! And take your money. We don't want or need your money! We take care of our own!"

I was saddened. I did not want to take my money. He lifted the envelope from the chess table and tossed it with authority. It hit me in the midsection. Instinctively, my hands wrapped around it.

Suddenly, he charged me. "You better hurry," he steamed. He grabbed my elbow. His grip was a vice of pain. "Before I change my mind." He pulled me closer so his face was right at mine. "I am only letting you go because I once loved my daughter..." then he whispered, "more than any-one knows." He thrust my elbow away from him and me along with it. "And don't come back."

He followed me to the door. He grabbed hold of the handle, opened it wide and gave me one last hard push as I was halfway through it. I found myself on the street beyond the outer wall of the grounds of the house.

"We hate Americans. I'll kill you next time." His voice seemed to ricochet off building brick throughout the town, as he pulled the thick teak door shut with a loud boom.

I looked about. Other people had noticed the interchange. I saw curious and stern reactions. His claims seemed well received by other Pakistanis. No witnesses appeared empathetic toward me.

Once on a different street, I hid my outer layer of funeral garb and the Kufi headwear under a bench. While periodically looking over my shoulder, I tried to approximate a saunter, as calmly and as quickly as I could. Near the ferry, jacaranda blossoms fell silently to the ground. Upward beyond the limbs rose resolutions of colors. I weighed heavy, thick with sorrow, but without regret, during the long slow push across the lake.

A Blue Note in the Key of C

I am always feeling blue as if my best girl has come home late and I don't know why and she won't tell me. It makes my heart ache as I fly through the air making my observations at the speed of sound, a blue note, a minor seventh in an F chord winging it in the key of C. That's me, born as a whining E flat just into the upper register of a wailing Buffet B flat clarinet scorching the bar with delirious unsettling troubling tones offering memories or feelings or contemplations some foreign and others too intense to sanely recollect. Like the woman below with rum and coke turned away from her date and crying silently, and he doesn't know that he cannot help her anymore because he keeps disappointing and although he loves her she knows he does not fit her anymore. At the moment she is crying because she used to love to listen to jazz with him, but this blues tune just turned her thoughts into a remorseful zone. She wiped the second tear from her eye so it too would not spill into her drink.

The table still close to the stage but at a slightly different trajectory, a person seems crushed from the inside out. He is wishing for peace knowing with certainty it will not arrive this night. He has tilted his head as if the minor seventh of the subdominant chord is what he thrives on at this very moment. He likes how long and with what feeling I've been bent by the moving embouchure of the musician, as I was squeezed out of the horn. He seems energized to have heard a sound so representing the sad state and confusion he has inside him that he cannot resolve and can barely describe. He had asked an acquaintance to join him this evening, but he only received a tentative reply and he knows what that normally means, disappointment. Oh, even if he had someone he could speak with, how would he know what to say? He only hoped the person might be able to bring something to the conversation so something beyond anything he could imagine might prevail, and with all this in his heart, he settled into me as I aligned with him so completely.

At a table a foot or two further away, sat a younger man nodding his head and gently waving his fingers over the table. He had told his friends he needed to hear some jazz, but I could tell he was uncomfortable with the blues because he was tapping his forefinger slightly off the beat. Although he seemed knowledgeable and as if he belonged perhaps more than anybody else in the bar, he was not enjoying himself, and when he heard me, he cringed, as if I drove him crazy, as if he had so much sadness in his heart, it was apparent he had not come to hear jazz, he had come to get away from something and hearing me just brought more pain to his soul, because he looked up at the ceiling and shook his head and yelled out, "Let's hear some upbeat riffs!" I felt sorry for him, because there is nothing as satisfying as the blues when one has settled into it, and nothing so annoying if you cannot absorb it. Fighting it was driving him crazy.

Just past him, a man wearing a beret and a woman with hair swept back were laughing. They had met in this very bar and tonight were celebrating and nodding in sync to the music. I savored their great appreciation of the blues. I watched as the man leaned over and kissed the woman gently on the cheek. They wrapped their arms around each other.

"My love," said the woman, "we're so lucky to feel the

same way we did way back when." He nodded and held her tighter.

"I love you even more, every year, every day, every hour. Do you want another drink?"

"No, this music has energized me. Let's take a walk home along the beach."

He gave her his hand, "I'd like nothing better."

A large round table, near the windows with a view of the ocean, many people sat together clinking glasses and making toasts to a friend. "To Bill, who did so much for all of us. He was among the kindest, smartest, most giving people I have ever known, and how he loved his family and his friends, and his *blues*!"

"To Bill!," someone else echoed.

I was floating past.

"The best father anyone has ever had!"

Nearer the window, another couple had wrapped themselves in a large fur blanket. They reacted to an F minor seventh, merely a distant calling, as they were in their own world, completely covered, with private caresses and words of whispered love dancing toward the end of the song.

Next to them a young woman who had just learned she was pregnant had a wistful, mysterious look. The young man with her had noticed, "Tell me whatever it is you're thinking about."

She answered, "The smooth, white sailing ships over the warm washing waves, and intertwined hugs overlooking the setting sun." Her face glowed with radiance.

"You're pregnant!" The young man clapped his hands joyfully.

Coincidentally, perhaps, when she heard me, she exclaimed, "Yes!"

Outside, an elderly woman, who could not afford to buy a drink, had set herself on a wooden crate and was smiling and welcoming me, as I lightly pierced her ear. She loved the blues. She loved me. Listening to jazz gave her such pleasure, in an otherwise difficult life. She had saved enough money to send her children off to college, but then the government had determined them to be untrue to the acceptable boundaries of the authoritarian regime. She was glad her daughter was out of the country and learning to use her mind. She was glad her son was working freely to better the world. She was so happy she had saved her children. She loved listening to jazz, and especially blues. She almost kissed me as I drifted faintly through the windows and down the street.

I had imagined troubles at other events and musical performances around the world. I thanked the magical puffs of melodic pheromones I was lucky enough to ride that evening without interference in this picturesque little Aptos village on the Central Coast where the worst thing I had to worry about was: When my gal came home late, would she once again refuse to tell me why?

The Confession

A large man with piercing brown eyes, cleared his throat. "First state your name."

The old man adjusted his glasses. "Are you the chief inspector?"

The large man observed sun-splotched hands tugging on a white beard. "Yes, I am."

"Okay then. My name's James Leopold Morgan."

"So what happened, Mr. Morgan?"

"From the beginning?"

"Yes. Everything."

It took the old man awhile to gather his thoughts. He shuffled about, until finally, he pulled himself up straight so he could rest his arms on the interrogation table. What follows is his statement:

Okay. First off, I left the garage. But I'd had a hard time starting the car. Rain pounded the convertible top. I turned onto Highway 68 and floored it. The wheels slipped, nearly skidding the Porsche Boxster off the asphalt. I wanted to get past the Salinas River before Cal Trans closed the highway or the car ran out of oil. Splashes of memories of this ride come to mind: the intersection at Canyon Del Rey and not wanting to wait for the red. There may have been a car crash and people beckoning me to pull over at the flooded entrance to Laguna Seca. It horrified me to see roadside bystanders near Monterey Creek Café fleeing like sandpipers or scattering like fish across both lanes and pointing in my direction. I lost control with the car spinning like a circus ride. Just caught a glimpse of "Danger Ahead", a warning sign? What danger? I saw none, driving full speed straight to where the freeway begins near Toro Park, swerving here and there and one time hitting something near the gun store, perhaps a trashcan. I remember thinking, I hope I didn't damage anything inside. The place has such a nice owner and such fair prices, a good place to buy a firearm. I may have even meandered along the sidewalk. I recall bits and pieces of water-streaked flickering lights through the city of Salinas, and suddenly the train station parking lot loomed in front of me, with a man in the car across from me shaking his fist, and I thought, 'Oh, no, not road rage! What could have caused that?' I grabbed my overnight bag and the envelope with my ticket and iPhone. I could not find Molly's reminder on the outside of the envelope. Funny, I think I, not she, packed the bag, and I managed to wear my most reliable security boots with their secret pouch of course. I slammed the Porsche door and hobbled as fast as I could, like an old wild dog fleeing a drooling predator, still shaking a fist and glaring at me and leaning out the driver-side door with his wife hanging onto his shirttail with both hands.

I searched through the station's popping colors and images. My eyes seemed on vacation. I wanted a clock and an arrival time for the train south.

Suddenly, I heard a voice. "Are you going to San Luis Obispo?" The question sounded like a command. I turned and the intense eyes of a thirty-something woman looked me down. I felt threatened. I feared she could send me through the air with a wicked wave of magic.

"I don't want to miss the train," I said. "Hospice called. My mother's dying."

"San Luis Obispo?"

"Yes, yes..."

"Here," she said. She jammed a package against my belly. "Take this. It needs to get to San Luis Obispo tonight."

In my mind I stammered, not sending meaningful words. "I don't want to miss the train." She seemed crazed, fiendish with determination. My eyes were blurring again, and my balance unsteady. Her demeanor or my exhaustion, perhaps both, had caused me to tremble.

"Here." She handed me several hundred dollars.

"What's that?" I demanded, "I 'm not working for you! Some hackneyed dangerous transaction! While you claim I will be safer than a butterfly!" My jumbled thoughts grabbed those insect ideas out of the air, namely how I loved the Monarchs. I always loved going over to Pacific Grove where they fluttered through those trees.

She grabbed me by the collar. "Put the package in your bag along with the money, and I'll walk you to the train."

I pulled myself free. Now dizzy, the walls began to rotate. I shrieked, "My mother's dying. I have to get there before she dies!" She took my bag and unzipped it. "Hey, what are you doing? I need that bag!"

"You do need that bag, and you also need money!" She glanced toward the outside platform.

My body shook from the heavy rumbling of the locomotive entering the station. I heard the loud deep voice announcing its arrival..."and continue on to San Luis Obispo in six minutes." Suddenly, I could not remember how I got to the station. I had questions. Had the hospice lady really called? Had mother lived long enough to be dying? If alive, how many years older than me? I seemed pretty old. Who had called me? I caught a reflection of an old bearded man in a framed elementary school watercolor painting hanging on the train station wall. Ancient! I wondered why he looked like me or I should say my father or grandfather. Suddenly, overcome with one desperate need above all others as I kept trying to remember the last time I had seen my mother, I stepped toward the bathroom. Immediately, I came to an abrupt halt by serious tugging on my arm. I turned. The same young woman with that crazed and determined face had an iron grip on my wrist. With my other hand I tried to remove myself from her.

"Where are you going?" she demanded. Such terror! I wondered how could anyone protect themselves from this woman?

"None of your business!" I shouted. When I tried to jerk my arm away again, pain shot through my wrist. The fingerized teeth had clamped down on my wrist tighter than ever. I leaned over close to her face and shouted as loud as I could, "I have to use the bathroom!"

Not at all intimidated, she moved closer and stared right back at me. "You need to get on that train to San Luis Obispo." She sounded like a prison guard. As an afterthought I guess, she stated, as if she were full of wonderful information, "They have bathrooms on the train." Then she added something I will never forget. "When you get on the train and go to the dining car, a woman will meet you and ask for your bag. Once you give it to her, she will take the package and will, in turn, give you ten thousand dollars which will be enough for you to get your Porsche fixed and also rent a car while it's in the shop."

How true were those words! My old 2003 Boxster. A financial nemesis, leaking oil like a sieve. But how did she know the cost of repairs? Forcefully, I strode toward the Men's Room, as she continued to hang on. I dragged her through the Men's Room door and right up to the urinal. People stared at us, and she just nodded and smiled as if she were my caregiver. The only time she let go, when I washed my hands. Then she handed me a paper towel.

When we left the Men's Room, the young woman hurried me through the waiting room past the ticket selling windows and outside across the platform toward the train to San Luis Obispo. She walked me up the stairs and inside a passenger car. She beckoned to the conductor, who approached us.

"This is Mr. Morgan. Like J. P. Morgan? He has an eating disorder, and he needs to go to the dining car and get a snack at one a.m. sharp."

I motioned toward the conductor. "I don't have an eating disorder." I stated it calmly, as one would who has complete control over his faculties.

He ignored me.

"And he needs to get exercise. He should not sleep; he also has a sleeping disorder!"

It shocked me to hear such lies. "I don't have a sleeping disorder!" I hollered.

The woman held out her card. "This should explain a few things," her tone and expression quite presumptuous.

The conductor read it aloud. "Senior Care Incorporated, Better Living For All." He turned to the woman. "We'll make sure he walks to the dining car at one a.m."

Once again, I screamed as loud as I could, "I don't have a sleeping disorder!"

The woman smiled at me. " Have a good trip, Mr. Morgan." I watched her turn and squirrel herself down the aisle away from me and the conductor. The conductor looked askance, as if I were a little kid. Depleted of energy and hope, I reached inside Molly's envelope for my ticket and gave it to him. The conductor took me by the arm and led me to my seat.

Like a grumbling giant, the clickety-clickety-clack and the hum of the wind and the rain and the storm rushed through me. The train bounded through unknown spaces. Its shrieks and shuhwish, shuhwish, shuhwishing sounds wore me out. Flashing orange and yellow strands of light accompanied the cacophonous chorus, so many unwanted intruders.

A ticket checker shook me awake. He started to lead me away. I recalled basic training in the Army. "Not without my bag!" We passed through several connectors to the dining car. A few people sat at tables. An elderly woman beckoned me to join her. She looked familiar. She asked me if I would like some pecan pie. I said I would. She nodded deliberately, as if she had known I loved pecan more than any other pie.

"Come on," she said. I followed her through several other connections to a sleeping car. We went inside and sat on a bed. She closed the door. I wondered what she had in mind. I did not see or smell any pecan pie. She reminded me of Molly. Perhaps Molly's sister? I hadn't seen her in years. Then I realized I did recognize her. For certain. She unzipped my bag and took out the package. When she opened it, I saw about a ream of documents.

She handed me a stack of money. "Your ten thousand dollars to fix your Porsche. Please just sign here, as a receipt to prove you received the money."

I took the money. "I can see you're Molly's sister Holly," I told her. "Do you know where Molly is?"

She studied me a moment. Believe it or not, she looked

like a cat figuring out the best way to trap her prey. "Jimmy, we can talk about everything, after you've signed the papers." She smiled as if to reassure me. I interpreted her smile as condescending. I remembered Molly had told me Holly could be like that.

I read a few parts of the documents to identify what they wanted me to sign. It had no resemblance to a receipt. I thought, 'Holy Moly!' It appeared I would be signing away my inheritance from Molly and giving it to her sister Holly. In name, I sounded wealthy, if you put the J.P. in front of the Morgan instead of James Leopold. In fact, Molly had brought more wealth to the marriage than I. Also, I relied on Molly and she relied on me. We would always remind each other, "One should never sign anything that didn't look right!" Of course, I had lost track of Molly's whereabouts. San Francisco? Visiting a cousin? Still alive? Anymore? My mind drew so many blanks. I recalled someone's funeral, could not separate out the details. I knew exactly where that cousin lived. I longed for Molly to join me. I missed her so much. I cleared my throat and faced Holly. I spoke with clarity. "I don't want to sign anything."

Holly took a deep breath and exhaled. "It will not be good for you, if you do not sign." Her eyes narrowed and she twitched her head, as if she were a member of a pack. I turned to see another person sitting on the bed behind me, a man, huge, masked, wild-eyed. He pulled a long-barreled pistol from a holster and began twisting a silencer into the barrel. He pointed it at my head, scaring me half to death.

I turned and faced Holly. I stated emphatically, "I will not be signing anything."

Suddenly, the silencer pushed against the back of my skull.

The gunman growled like a monster, "You'll sign or this will be the last thing you remember."

Thoughts inside my head clamored like bells clanging in my brain. They ricocheted like an explosion, and I began to cry. Tears flowed down my cheeks. I went into my biggest act. I can cry at the drop of a hat. "Ow! My leg! When I'm under stress, I get this pain in my foot. It's killing me! I'll sign. I'll sign, but first I need to rub my foot!"

As I sobbed right in front of those bullies. I looked back at the man and then to Holly, who smirked like the Russians refusing to negotiate and bragging about how they're winning the war. She did not hide her contempt for my weakness. "Let him rub his damn foot."

I could hardly breathe. I leaned down to rub my leg. Definitely scared, my shaking hands personified the term *quaking in his boots.*" I dug into the soft leather of my favorite footwear and found the pocket with the 9mm pistol Molly always warned me never to carry. "Oh, that feels better," I said as I continued to sob.

"If it feels better," demanded Holly, " it's time to sign the damn papers!"

The man with the gun at the back of my head was right. Like the Ukrainians unexpectedly blowing up 7 billion dollars' worth of jets in the middle of the Soviet Union, I heard two shots, and that was the last thing I remembered. Oh, except for this. With the two of them lying there, I saw the apparition of my grandfather outside the charging train, his face clearly lit by the overhead bulb inside the sleeper, but more like a spotlight. He had lived in a violent era back at the turn of the previous century. Posturing like a judge and jury, from the other side of the window, his smile as broad as baby's, singing, 'You righted that wrong! And it was self-defense!" Then, as he tilted his gray head back and laughed, a jolt of lightning revealed a happy surprise. Beside him, Molly—the picture of eloquence with her heavenly blue gown flowing softly over her—floated in the air serene as an angel in the raging, stormy night, and next to her my mother, softly whispering so I could clearly hear, "I love you, son." I will remember that scene and those words for the rest of my life. I wish you could have observed all I saw."

The large man with piercing brown eyes nodded. "And that's your full confession?"

"Yes. That's all there is to it, self-defense. Just like I said. Any of them, Molly, mom, my granddad, they will verify everything."

The large man gently laid his hands on the old man's shoulders. "That's quite a tale." He helped the old man stand. "Obviously, self-defense. You fought a good fight. Protected your assets. You are my granddad, and I'm proud of you. How about we celebrate with some pecan pie?"

"As long as you believe I'm innocent."

"One hundred percent."

"Okay," said the old man. He shuffled a few feet." Only, how were they just flying through the air outside the train's window?"

The large man took some time to contemplate as he guided his grandfather's elbow. "That's a real mystery. But they are your witnesses. No matter how they did it, they can prove your innocence."

The old man smiled, appreciating his grandson's affirmation. "I guess I'll have my dessert a la mode."

Christmas in Soho

December 22, 1974, an American, alone, visiting London, I had taken my horn around to different places. Back home, I had sat in with Jake Stock and the Abalone Stompers both in the bowling alley in Monterey and at the River Inn at Big Sur. Jake, a very kind man, would say, "Stick around, kid, you can take a few licks near the end of the night."

I loved it. I would put the five pieces of the licorice stick together and soak my reed and wait for my opportunity. Sometimes I got up to forty minutes. I always admired the trumpet player, forget his name. He rolled through his solos so brilliantly, so much smoother than I. Feeling grateful to Jake, I never did become as good as he, but little by little I did improve. Those experiences helped prepare me to ask to sit in with a couple of jazz groups in Soho until I landed a one-night job playing blues and traditional jazz and even a few Christmas carols. Their clarinet had left town for a couple of days.

Not being a Brit and not being that familiar with the British jazz scene, I listened heavily with my fingers dancing lightly over the keys and continually adjusting to the present moments of the evening's improvisational expressions. Other players gave me some leeway, as everyone knew an unknown person sitting-in would be scrambling and adjusting, a foreigner to their distinctive musical culture. Yet, working to find a strand of comfort in each of the group's songs and trying to align with the styles of each of the other players, though challenging and all encompassing, did not take the prize for the evening's most revelatory experience.

Ours, the early set, we finished around 8 pm. Self-critical as always, I thought I could have played better and I wondered should they even pay me, but they did. Graciously, they spoke kind words regarding my performance and even asked how to get in touch with me, should they need me again. Unfortunately, I had no response, as my plans were fluid. I knew I would be visiting family friends in the UK. Free to travel when and where I liked, and I had the urge to move along, unless they had other work pending, a possible reason to stay. The trumpet player asked me if I wanted to get a drink, and I said sure. Outside, I shook hands with the others. We all hoped we would meet up again.

Rick, the trumpet player, caught my attention. "I know this pub," he said. "I go there all the time."

"Sure," I said.

We headed through some darker streets. I could see the name, The Lyrics, the pub's corner building lit-up with signs and windows inside and out. "So, Marshal, where about do you live in the states?"

"California."

"San Francisco. L.A.?"

"Carmel. You been there?"

"When I was in the merchant marines we stopped at Monterey once. Forget why. I saw the Lone Cypress Tree." He stopped and thought a moment. "And there was L.A. L.A. had those riots. In Watts."

I remembered that so well. "Terrible. Mobs in the streets, fires everywhere, bricks tossed over bridges..."

Rick nodded seriously. "Yes, I didn't think much about it at the time." He smiled and nodded his head. "But later I did."

I just nodded and sighed heavily. I had lived in L. A. back

then, in fear, afraid to drive through some parts of Los Angeles, especially at night. "I was a student. We thought civil rights was going in the right direction, but then, clearly, it wasn't."

Rick stopped on the street across from the pub. "You have anything against black people?"

"Not at all."

"You have any black friends?"

"I don't know many black people."

Rick nodded. "You want to meet some?"

"Sure," I said.

"I'm married to a Jamaican woman, met her on the way back to port. Fell for her. Flew back to Kingston, took a while to woo her. Her folks weren't much for the English."

"Sounds like an amazing story."

"She's the love of my life. We're catching up at a dance hall just around the corner. Could be a little later, or you and I could go right now."

I knew not what to expect. Momentarily, I surprised myself that along with anticipation of a new experience, fear had filled my head. Even so, I had just played jazz with my new friend and I uttered the words without a thought. "I'd like that."

It did not take us long to ramble through more dimly lit passageways, until we came to a long, flat sided building, stretching with small high windows along a narrow sidewalk.

"Here we are." Rick opened the door to the large foyer. "Come on."

I followed him across the width to where a black man stood. He wore a large floppy brimmed hat, green flowing shirt, and beige flowing trousers, as if he were about to take his celebration to the dance floor. "Ciao, Rick." The man looked me over.

"Ciao, Rushawn. Oh yah. He's with me."

"Steady as she goes," said Rushawn.

Inside, the wooden floor spread out to become a grand hall, large enough to house a few hundred people. Maybe two hundred were dancing and milling about. Momentarily, it took me back to years before, just after the Watts Riots. As a UCLA student, I wanted to do something to heal the violence between races. UCLA provided two buses to Watts. Upon arrival, all of us students were herded into a hall or a theater with a proscenium framing the stage from where we were supposed to receive an explanation for the work or tutoring we would be doing in the black community. Through hanging curtains entered a black man wearing shirt, pants, and shoes akin to army fatigues and striding as if he were about go after someone. He took the microphone from the stand in the center of the stage and he scanned the young white faces. He caught my eye for a moment, as he caught the eyes of so many others.

He held the microphone close to his mouth and moved forward, toward us, then back and forth as he emphasized his words, "You white liberal youngsters are here because you want to save the world, but you need to know, nobody wants you here. Nobody wants what you think you have to give. We don't want to learn all about your white ways. You are not the ones to teach us how to think or about what to think. We don't want your salvation. We don't want to learn about your majoritarian culture. If you have come here to save black kids, if you have come here to teach black kids white ways, the ways you have learned to succeed, and you think that is what everyone here needs to learn, well you can turn right around on those buses and don't come back."

My immediate reaction had been fear. Suddenly, I realized black people did not trust me and did not like me, no matter what my intentions. I had never before considered, how I had been living, with whom I had been living, and for what beliefs I had been living, in fact, just being true to myself could cause me as a person to be totally offensive or even disdained by some other group, race or culture of people. The fear I learned in that theater continued for years and still lingered within me as I entered the dancehall in Soho and saw only dark faces except for one other white person in the entire dancehall.

I had to consciously address my panic. I commanded myself to relax. I told myself to cherish this important new learning, in the line of many new learnings, to allow it, like all of the others, to play out. I took a deep breath, I looked about and felt my tension ebb. I observed the atmosphere, the casual, friendly nature of all the people and felt uplifted. Obviously, most in attendance had previously been acquainted. I opened my heart to what I saw, a room so filled with laughter and light conversations. Everyone dressed in array of colors and styles, some as if from Jamaica or Africa, Asia, or America, seemed confident and caring. I allowed myself to absorb the collective aura. Twenty or thirty people danced in different places along the wood.

A tall, friendly woman danced up to Rick, "Hello, you," she said.

"Hello, love." The way they hugged and kissed, one could tell their love carried deep friendship and mutual respect, as if they had a habit of fun and enjoying time together in the present tense.

Rick motioned to me, "Tianna, this is Marshal. He's from California."

Tianna's smile broadened, open and full of trust. "Hello, Marshal, welcome to Soho." She hugged me on the right and then the left.

My heart melted with gratitude for her unqualified warmth. "Hello, Tianna, it is my pleasure."

"Come on, then." She took my hand and led me along with Rick across the wood to a group of her friends.

"This is Rick's friend, Marshal. I'd like you to meet some very special people..."

I have no idea if Tianna had a clue as to the profound changes she had allowed to transform inside me. Rarely have I ever felt more welcome than I did that night. Even as I danced with each of Tianna's friends to another reggae song wondering about my movement or how I stepped, somewhere I stopped worrying about doing everything wrong and I just started doing. And somewhere I stopped worrying about how probably if everyone knew I came from a white majoritarian culture, they would probably dislike and distrust me, and instead I just began to relax and think of myself as another one of all the other unique people in the dancehall who were also just having fun. As if rinsing and washing my soul, I embraced this brief glimpse into a world where humans love and experience joy without hindering the kaleidoscopic brilliance celebrating diversity of skin and culture. I saw the evening filled with poignant lessons for a giving Christmas season.

Tianna asked me to dance on the last song of the evening, Dennis Brown singing reggae, "Westbound Train." Some of the lyrics were of a lover saying she will never ever see him again. I wondered if Tianna could sense how my heart had continued to open over so little time. When the song had finished and everyone applauded the end of a grand evening, she gave me a hug and quietly spoke into my ear, "Marshal, I hope you won't be riding that westbound train. I hope we will be seeing you again."

I had no idea when I would be able to return to England. I simply replied, "I hope to get back here. You and Rick will be in my heart forever."

Brightness in the Early Evening Shadows

The morning loomed over the city like a heavy wake. Karl could hardly breathe, his eyes full of tears, his mind reeling with regrets. How had he been separated from Sarah? Once again the young woman's scream, jammed with fear, rose like a distant whisper from the broken tunnels of debris. Somewhere he envisioned her trapped on a floor of liquid muck surrounded by darkness. Listening to falling chimney brick and shaken by rumblings of aftershocks, he could almost hear the mocking of wooden beams and girders, and the hissing of collapsed walls of cement, iron, wood, and plaster. Unhinged by isolation, as if harvested by fiendish spirits, thickening fog sealed him from his love. He dove head-on with resolve. He crashed through the debris. He pushed through pain and fear, pressurized by diminishing time and increasing hazard. He manufactured strength from exhaustion, adrenaline pumping, to rise against the resounding ring of evil attempting to devour human sensations. He had recognized the identity of the woman making the desperate calls for help.

He tore into the jagged crawlspace, a blackened hole from whence the woman's cries had emanated. His gloveless hands followed the maze of options as he squeezed deeper without being able to see. The crushing weight of worry masked how to make where she was safe. He would not be able to find his way back. Fire cinders hushed by mud stole air from his lungs. He scrambled through a section strewn with bits of fallen chimney, upright iron rods poking out of broken bricks. On bloody hands and achy legs, he followed the precarious short tunnel and scooted to an open pocket of large beams, headers and girders jutting into each other at different angles up from the hungry soggy ground. The open ends of wood tenuously supported one another, finally, for him, a lonely section of hope.

The pungent smokey air hungered for his strength. The woman had stopped screaming. He called out, "Sarah! It's me, Karl! Where are you?"

A desperate voice responded. "Here! I'm over here!"

The pain in his chest tore almost beyond tolerance. Karl's head swelled with tears and determination. "Sarah!" He could hear as Sarah began to sob.

"Karl? How did you find me?"

"Hang on, my love. I'm going to help you get out of here!"

Her continued sobbing deepened his distress, to get so close and not to have his arm around her. He envisioned tight irregular paths through the unstable maze from where he presumed her voice had emanated. He now pushed through the demon scum. He heard loud cracking overhead. Dark forces had twisted the building to prevent Karl from reaching the woman he loved. He could see the floorboard monsters laughing and dancing and chewing their cuds, ready to come crashing down; and, as if from the bowels up through the throat of the carnivore, he could smell the putrid kitchen grease. He pushed between the thick wooden timbers, precariously hanging by damaged metal straps and twisted bolts. He used a four-by-four to poke through the darkness. "Sarah, let me know where you are!" he hollered.

"Here! I'm over here!"

He found an opening in the mud that allowed him to crawl a quick twenty feet. The rancid smell of burning oil overwhelmed him. He heard increased creaking as the building continued to shift.

"Can you reach me?" Her voice held hope.

Through the haze he could just make out her figure. "I'm gonna get to you. Hang on." He charged harder through fallen debris, until smoke fumes blocked his vision and his breathing. Something crashed hard against the top of his head. "Sarah?" he called out.

"Karl?" Her question became a hideous scream, "Karl!!!"

He opened his mouth. He could not get enough air to make a sound. Desperation enveloped him like a strait jacket.

The discordant collapse of the building rumbled like thunder. The massive wild arms of destruction pounded them like a mob of hellhounds. He attempted one last holler, "Sarah!!" His whisper did not convey sound. He could not catch any air. He could not move and pain embroiled him. Everything went black. His brain slid into death.

Now in utter darkness, he screamed louder than he could ever remember screaming. He awoke and jerked upright in bed.

Karl's eyes popped open. In a sweat, he tried to focus, as if searching for an anchor. He remembered! His hotel room, high ceiling, long blackout curtains, dark wooden credenza, he had flung his pants over a tall leather chair. These observations procured his reality, one of the boxing coaches for the US Olympic team, in Paris, 1924 and not someone recovering bodies inside San Francisco buildings broken by the harrowing quake of 1906, as he had once done.

He had fear. Often his dreams allowed him to see into the future. In one, his mother and he had been riding horses over the plains, a joyous race filled with laughter. They approached a cliff. He pulled on his reigns. She did not. His horse stopped. Hers cantered over the edge. He watched her fall, accelerated by the power of gravity, until, as if by magic, she and her favorite mare began floating. They floated into the air and disappeared over the horizon. Subsequently, he learned his mother had died earlier in the day.

Now he wondered about Sarah. Had Sarah become involved in some danger? She had been on business to the UK. Recently, a boat train had crashed in northern France. Because of that accident, Karl suggested Sarah fly between London and Paris, but as she said, they had only been flying that route since August of 1919, a mere five years. She preferred a more established manner of travel.

* * *

From the moment Sarah waved good-bye to her editor and entered the boat train to begin her return to France, she looked forward to the luxurious ride to Dover, the crossing to Calais, then another boat train to Paris. She had been in London for two days. Her publisher had great plans for what Sarah had written, and Sarah celebrated those plans for her book with a group of editors at the publishing house. Now, she looked forward to a relaxing trip getting back with Karl in Paris. The channel had flat swells. The afternoon train to Paris soothed her energies as she let herself listen to the rhythmic motion of those wheels. She sensed a calmness, even a meditative spirit. When she entered the dining car, she requested a table by the window where she could sit alone. Sarah personified intellect and style . The maître 'd nodded to her, "Mais oui, Madame." With grace, she followed him as he affected her request.

Sometime later, as she anticipated the waiter bringing her food, she noticed a man eyeing her from some distance across the dining car. She ignored him and turned her attention to the window. From a momentary glance, she had seen the deep eyebrows, heavy beard, mustache, and full head of wavy black hair. A thick gold chain dangled from the breast pocket of his expensive double-breasted suit. He had eyes of someone who did not like to hear *no* for an answer. She hoped he would not join her, but the table had four places, and even though she had requested a private table, the culture of the dining car commanded sharing.

"Do you mind if I join you?" he said.

"Are you sure there is not somewhere else you would rather sit?"

Her comment seemed to surprise him, as if he may have thought she had been rude, but he smiled and his eyes liberally ran over her visage. "Yes, I am quite sure."

Disappointment. Sarah often ignored insulting lures, and she had no patience to endure the boring, arrogant men who had convinced themselves they were so entitled to propagate such rude advances. "I will be leaving soon," she replied.

She thought perhaps she had a slight chance to continue enjoying her afternoon, and so once again, she looked away and peered out the window as the train continue rushing by lovely pastoral scenes. When she heard the man clear his voice, as if to speak, she turned further away and bowed her head closer to the paper as if she had found some article of interest, then she slid the paper closer toward the window.

"What a beautiful day, eh? A perfectly romantic day of fun. And to think I have the good fortune to be sitting across from such a beautiful stranger, someone I would very much love to get to know better!"

She made certain her eyes would give him no encouragement. "I am married and traveling to Paris to be with my husband."

The man laughed. "How many women have said something like that to me? Not too many after they learn the fun they can have with me. What's your name?"

Sarah lifted the paper to her face and turned a page. She continued to read, blocking herself from his eyes.

The man laughed. "That's what I like, a challenge!"

His proclamation declared the beginning of deaths. The death of a charming afternoon. The death of a beautiful meal. The death of a celebratory ride. The death of feeling free enough for beautiful anticipations of being with Karl. Even though her food had only arrived and she had not eaten a bite, she folded the paper into a tight roll and waved it high in the air to catch the waiter's attention. As he approached, the bearded man interrupted.

"Oh, I'll get it, Jacque!"

Right away, Sarah stood and twisted the paper tighter, "No, Jacque!" She put a twenty-franc note in Jacque's hand. "I'm paying! And keep the change!"

Jacque looked frightened now and turned toward the bearded man, as he continued to block her escape.

Suddenly, Sarah lifted the paper and swatted the waiter hard on the shoulder as if he were infested with bugs. "Let me by, Jacque! You're in my way!"

Some of the other passengers could now hear her raised voice and were glancing in Sarah's direction. Finally, the bearded man nodded for Jacque to step aside, and he did.

As Sarah walked past, the bearded man added a warning, "I am one of the owners of this train. There's nowhere you can hide. I can always find you."

Once Sarah reached her private storage space, she gathered her case, organized her private items, and quickly and methodically began searching the first-class passenger compartments until she found one solely occupied by women.

She did not want the man's threat to hang like a bludgeon over her remaining trip, including transferring in Paris to the subway enabling her to reunite with Karl.

Conversation in this new compartment had ceased, as Sarah stepped over legs and cases. One woman had to remove a package from the last remaining seat.

"*Excusez moi*," said Sarah.

A second woman had a look of concern as she watched Sarah sit. "Are you all right, madam?"

Sarah glanced at the group of eyes, from one to the other, all sympathetic. She guessed her preoccupations had shown through. These appeared to be young professional women. She thought they could be empathetic, so she continued in French. "I'm taking refuse from a stalker, rude and forward, even with the knowledge I have given him, that I am on my way to meet my husband."

The woman sitting between her and the window grunted knowingly. "What's he look like?"

"It's not so much what he looks like, but his attitude. He claims to be an owner of this railroad."

Several women chuckled. "We know him," someone said. All agreed. The woman between her and the window added, "He won't let up. He'll be by. He will ask us to move. We won't move. Tell us about your husband."

Sarah thought about Karl, caring, loving, strong, the only man she ever had known with whom she had complete freedom to be herself. He respected her opinions and solutions. He often expressed appreciation or even intrigue when he learned of the experiences and reflections from which her perspectives had derived. He collaborated well. While extolling her talent, he made core questions and suggestions about what he had read often pinpointing what she needed to consider to improve a piece.

Sarah smiled and sighed. "I would, but if I did, all of you would want to take him away from me." The other women laughed.

The stalker did open the door to the compartment. He offered tickets for any of the women to upgrade to the diner or to the upper deck. As he spoke, Sarah wrapped a hand around the sharpest pencil in her bag. The women, true to their word, did not allow him entry; and with him looking on, all disembarked together and strode to where Sarah would pick up the subway to Hotel de Ville.

Karl, still worrying about what truths his dream might have foreshadowed, paced back and forth keeping his eye on the main exits of the subway station. Suddenly, Sarah appeared. She hesitated on the corner sidewalk and looked about.

Relieved, he hurried toward her.

She saw him and quickened her step toward him.

In the bustle of an overcast evening, Karl caught her in stride and lifted her high. To him, she felt so alive. To her, he felt so strong. Slowly, their lips locked in their passion.

Onlookers, thinking about getting home after a day of work and scurrying right along, seemed not to notice, even as the pair created such a spectacular brightness in the early evening shadows.

Rain

The mind, the body, the soul, love, the emotions...how intricately interwoven when unbeknown to us one or more begin to fall. How do we extricate one from the other? When do we know when we have lost one and if one collapses do they all? Not always? Under conditions rippling violently like an undulating storm, which elements of mind, emotion, and body can one salvage? How long does one gamble trying to save all while losing oneself, before deciding to save oneself? This was not a shipwreck but a marriage. Why should one respond differently to one over the other? Like a ship, marriage depends on the amount of wreckage as well as the distance from port. I have introduced here more than I could answer and because of my limitations I pondered these questions through years of decline. Now I ask, knowing the full extent of the successes and the failures: What prevented me from doing a better job analyzing truths and confusion obscuring those truths? I had concluded the only solution was to leave many times. That I did not was a kind of betrayal, or was it? I believe only if we are true to ourselves can we represent what is fundamental to happiness and life. I do not believe: if life is the struggle for survival—of the soul, of the mind, of the body, of the emotions—then rising up out of hard conditions and tragedy must make for the best teacher. To gain the energy to struggle, don't we all need the foundation developed during harmonious continuums, don't we need to know joy or at least peace of mind as a frame of reference? I wondered where that was. How does one learn to overcome turmoil while being inundated and controlled by it? When one is in it, how does one find the answers to these questions? I was in it, and I did not know the answers to these questions.

So when she said she only wanted to stay at the Ritz, my subconscious rose up and reminded me of my pain and perennial questioning. "How can you change everything out of the blue, after all the energy we've put into planning our new beginning?" Her quick and flippant answer arrived carefully considered and only seemingly off the wall.

"I wasn't talking about the penthouse, and only for two nights, so we can rest up before you drive me to the Riviera."

Another flash illuminating the interwoven threads circuitously winding through the mysterious dilemma of why we remained together: Was I masochistic, empathetic, or ignorant beyond belief, and how much was I capable of enduring, giving, loving, forgiving and resolving? How much emotional energy and understanding did I have? What did I know about the balance of all the factors, the needs of love for each individual, including the position of truth, versus the survival of deception and lies and the manufacture of twisted emotional intrigue and the fabrications of emotional pain leading to weird celebrations of twisted superficial resolutions? Would she have tormented me beyond belief only to have that agony topped off with love making, as a reward, once we arrived in the room on the 8th floor of the Ritz?

"I won't be camping," she said. "Or spending nights in this van."

"But you and I agreed, that's the only way we can afford a year in Europe."

"You'll find a way for us to finish out the year."

So said the expert on the secrets of emotional motivation,

including the strands and designs of emotional operations we always seemed to be riding. I did not question my lack of understanding related to many of her responses and actions, since I considered myself somewhat ignorant in this part of my being. For the longest time, I trusted her blindly, her explanations of other peoples' secret motives and justifications. So often we argued about what I did not know. It did occur to me, at one point, how often we might have been talking or operating, perhaps intentionally, I only guessed, in some respects on different levels. I did not reflect, until later, the consideration our connection had been steered into destruction by lack of self-efficacy, although from uniquely different aspects both hers and mine. I had pulled off to the side of the road. We had only just left Germany.

"I can't. We don't have the funds. I tell you what, let's split the money we've saved for our trip. You take the van and I'll buy camping gear and hoof it."

"No!" she screamed. "You're going to drive me to the Riviera!"

It became an argument placing no value on sound reasoning, until she flung the travel book into the back of the van. "I've had it with you. You're impossible! Just send me back to the States."

I watched her plane rise into the distance and disappear behind the clouds before I turned to find the van. Peculiarly and unexpectedly, I felt one emotion stronger than all others: Relief. I moved, walked, drove, ate, spoke as if functioning underwater and breathing as if by snorkel. Overwhelmed with gratitude to something unseen within myself which had forced me to separate from the woman I had thought I loved, I found myself crying with tears of remorse and happiness.

Later when lonely, I thought it a small price to pay for the possibility of peace of mind.

During the following two and a half months, I drove to England and travelled from one campsite to another, reflecting and jotting down thoughts, awkwardly analyzing aspects of our lives, including the causes of the demise of two high school sweethearts whose families were so close, as well as actions and attitudes I could change to cope with and prevent more heartbreak in the future. It confused me, even with all the heavy downward feelings shedding light on how we ruined everything, some other inner voice wanted to set aside our tormented and depressed state and entertain some weird compulsion I should want to find a way to begin again, even if it meant reestablishing the craziness. I ate only when hungry and dropped fifteen pounds. I went to sleep only when spent, and I awoke fresh and eager for the unknown prospects of each new day. I energized myself with walks and excursions. I took time to enjoy and absorb the characteristics distinct to the British people, the architecture, the countryside, the bustle of the cities.

I began to uncover structure to the patterns of our perennial nose-diving spirals, and it showed much of our problems derived from us just not fitting. These revelations allowed healing from all our battles to begin. I did not miss the turmoil, the drinking, and the lies. Nor did I miss the sessions of psychologists' plans for promises and solutions, always shattered by further falsehoods and disappointments. I began to wonder did anyone have a relationship without continual emotional storms? Every day I concentrated on my renewal. I had refused to address the needs of warmth and human touch. Searching for relevant reflections and answers to find a balanced state drove my days.

It had been raining hard for almost a week. I loved the rain. I loved to walk in it and hear it patter against my poncho and against my hat. But it had rained so much, keeping a dry pair of shoes and continually washing and drying clothes became regular.

I settled in a wooded campsite on the outskirts of London. When the weather cleared, I laid out a plastic tarp on the water-soaked ground and gained immense pleasure from the sun's warmth. The trees grew tall and formed natural boundaries for the sites. The different green hues in the trees, shrubs, and grass all seemed fresh and clean making dramatic contrasts with the browns in the darkened soil and the rain-soaked bark of the overhanging limbs and the soaring canopies. The air twittered melodically with the whistling of birds.

Other campers took advantage of the respite to clean gear and walk about. Two men deepened the drainage ditch around the periphery of their tent. An elderly woman with a small child washed mud from a tarp. I had parked on a hill overlooking the main part of the woods. While writing, reflecting, trying to figure things out, I remember how it brought peace of mind to observe the harmonious activity of those few who had camped outside in spite of the rain.

A young woman came from a knoll to my right and walked down the gentle grade toward the restrooms and office. I had overlooked her two-person tent, even though it sat nearby. It's brown exterior blended nicely with the earthen hill behind it. For a moment I watched her, a new character in the moving pictorial below me. Her bulky clothes made her appear storm ready. She passed near me on the return. I said hello. She smiled and declined to reply. At the time, I thought nothing of her lack of response, I was so deep into my unraveling thoughts. Later, when I finished polishing my boots, I saw her again, in the laundromat.

"Hello," I said.

"Allo."

Surprised she answered me, I put down my note pad. "Where are you from?"

"Belgium. You're an American."

"Yes. I'm Ben."

"Jeanne-Marie."

We spoke easily while we washed and dried our clothes. I asked if she would like to join me for a cup of coffee. She said she would.

We sat at the table that swung up from the van's exterior. After so many inclement days, the instant coffee had an aroma like the best Columbian home ground. A drizzle had begun ahead of the prognosis for even more rain. We discovered shared interests in hiking and bicycling. She asked if I could speak French, but my French, inferior to her English, encouraged continuation in English. She removed her hood. She had the face of a pixie, rosy cheeks and fine white skin. Her eyes danced as if she were about to try out a joke, as if life were presentations of joyful opportunities. Her hair curled in wavy layers, falling almost to her shoulders.

"I attend university in Brussels. Also, I'm mistress to an older man, an architect. And you," she said. "What about you?"

I allowed myself to appreciate her candor. "First of all, I'm married."

She laughed. "You're very honest."

"As were you."

She acknowledge my comment with a nod. "Where is your wife?"

"California, the Central Coast. We separated a few months back."

"I'm sorry to hear. Break-ups are so often painful."

I nodded in agreement.

"Is it permanent?"

I thought a moment. "I really don't know."

She waited. "So often hard to know."

"And you?" I asked. "Are you in love with the architect?"

She replied without a moment's thought. "He is someone I like a lot." She smiled and shrugged. "I think I better leave before it begins to rain."

At night, several hours after Jean-Marie had departed, torrents of rain, more threatening perhaps than anything over the past several days, began pouring down. It pleased me to hear it pound so dramatically outside on the roof of the van, while I lay happily and calmly inside dry and warm. The rain and the social interaction with campers crystalized some of my thinking. I found and wrote clear ideas defining reasons for failed solutions in my marriage.

About four in the morning I awoke from a rap-tap on the door. Through the screen, I saw Jeanne-Marie, looking as if she had fallen into a river while wearing her clothes. She smiled. "May I come in?"

"Yes," I said. I put on shorts and opened the door. I extended a hand for her to grab so her wet shoes would not slip climbing the stairs. "Let me get you a towel."

Energetically, she rubbed her soaking wet hair with the thick terrycloth. I put a blanket over a line between the high backs of the front seats so she could have some privacy.

"My tent just collapsed, it rained so hard."

I nodded. "Yeah, it's really coming down." She seemed empty-handed. "Do you have some dry clothes?"

"Sort of, a shirt."

I held out another pair of my shorts. "This might work. It has a tie string."

"Oh, thanks," she said.

I could hear the thud of her wet garments hitting the floor in front of the passenger seat, as she freed herself from her outer layers. I retrieved a sweatshirt. "And take this. It's big, but..."

She glanced back at me with an appreciative smile. Her hand reached alongside the blanket. "Maybe I could spend the night, at least until I can get another tent..."

"Sure."

The next day the sun came out. I drove Jeanne-Marie to a camping supply store where she purchased a new tent. She pitched it in a slightly different location. She claimed she enjoyed her isolation and independence.

We became good friends, hiked and biked together and shared ideas about our different cultures and relationships. We travelled to Wales for several intimate weeks.

Even though her world seemed so much more complex than mine, she thought of life as simple, living in the present, experiencing whatever came next. Her philosophy affected me in a positive manner and enabled me to compose a number of essays about new revelations based on our discussions.

It had taken months to once again feel light-hearted and free. For the first time in a long while, I could live in the present without unexplained negative residue tugging on my heart.

I could go on and on conveying the years of a life well lived, but I have not written this story for me. I have written it for you, my friend and reader. You, like me, I suspect, are touched by the decisions lovers make about their lives causing helpful or harmful results in the name of love. Who among you has not overlooked some minor injury allowed to fester longer than you would have preferred? What meditations, decisions, and actions would bring enough presence for you and your lover to enjoy the pitter-patter sounds of rain?

When The Saints Go Marching In

In his eighth decade, Malcolm had been floundering, lonely and seemingly without purpose, yet today he found himself wondering how so often the best things, people and experiences came to each of us when we had done nothing to earn them and had no anticipation of them. More importantly, what caused these tangles in the universe, the whys and wheres and whens, the comportment of the unknown to suddenly lean into peoples' lives, especially in joyful ways? Of course everyone knew all too well about all the other ways. Occasionally, over the period of his life, Malcolm may have hoped for new beginnings, but he had never organized one with 100 percent success to prevent unwanted continuations of the negative agitations inherent in the need for change. Only fate or the unseen had presented newness with boundless joyous freedom. He wondered, dare he hope, could this happen again? He heard the woman clear her throat. He drew comfort from her smiling face.

"Let me show it to you."

June lived in the English countryside with her husband, Arnold, some forty miles north of London. She knew how almost everyone reacted when they saw their special little place. This man, Malcolm Jones, had no idea how his life would change as he became an integral part of their family. She and Arnold chose to implement a plan, born from chance, circumstance, and love, and they hoped the hourglass would clog just a bit so they could take these actions before the sand ran out. What a coincidence to have run into Malcolm at Tristan's fundraiser celebrating the fiftieth anniversary of his father, Kenneth Allsop, saving Dorset from the oil drillers and so many others. June and her husband Arnold were huge proponents of environmental protection and had been heavily influenced by Kenneth Allsop.

June led Malcolm out the back door, past the side garden and around a flowering hedge. There she stopped and swung open her arm as if to accentuate the presentation. It pleased her to see his reaction, as he followed her gaze.

Malcolm stopped and stared, awestruck by the cottage, a blanched Lime-cliffs colored stucco with dramatic thatched roof, standing gently and surprisingly like a Mozart etude at the edge of her property, surrounded by trees with a creek running nearby. Inside a small kitchen introduced a sitting room with a fireplace. The light entering through the open shutters washed a piano and the room in a dreamy, hopeful aura. Upstairs, the bed and bathroom vistas spanned the creek, the drive, the main house, and beyond. For months, maybe years, Malcolm had felt loss and no peace, and now a change came, a calm swell above his diaphragm, reminding him of a small child playing with harmonies, if not free of life's agonies, perhaps swallowing them.

"You can stay for as long as you like."

The words swished through the air like a life saver. "I know you told me that. We don't even know each other." Malcolm inhaled deeply. He wondered why anyone who resided in this cottage would ever want to leave. "It's too much, too kind."

"No." June tugged gently on Malcolm's elbow. "My husband and I have given this a lot of thought. You are going to teach our grandson about music, and we get to listen."

"Okay. Yes. It's a wonderful offer. But I can only do what

WHEN THE SAINTS GO MARCHING IN 127

I do." Malcolm, struck by the look on her face filled with so much trust and kindness, intuited something else. She appeared to have a thorough understanding of her actions, him coming together with this cottage by the fruition of careful planning.

The next day, at the scheduled time, Malcolm heard a knock, knock. When he opened the door, there stood June next to her grandson, Winston, eleven years old. June had summarized the problem. Malcolm wanted to hear it for himself. He asked June if she wanted to stay. She declined with a wink, calmly explaining she had no desire to impede the progress.

Malcolm thought Winston might one day grow into his name, but at this stage he seemed vulnerable like an uncurling leaf. "Do your friends all call you Winston?"

The boy stood erect and pushed the clarinet into the air. "Sometimes someone will try Winnie, but they only do that once because this is what they get." Two more times he pumped his fist holding the clarinet.

Malcolm nodded. He wondered when Winston would grow enough to respect the precise nature of the adjustments on the keys enabling a person to play the horn with maximum efficiency. "Well, your grandmother says your clarinet teacher claims you're quite good."

"I hate it. I hate playing the clarinet. I also hate playing the piano. I bloody hate both of them."

Such proclamations! Malcolm thought it likely he would have success teaching this kid. "You know I play the clarinet."

"Mum told me."

"I love it."

"To repeat...I don't fancy it at all."

Malcolm paused with a concerned respectful demeanor. "What is music to you?"

"A bunch of notes on a page some pedant deemed fit to practice."

Malcom smiled. He recalled when his younger self had reached a similar conclusion. "What if you could learn to play what you want and even make up new stuff you like?"

"Brilliant." Winston rolled his eyes and flopped his mouth wide open. "How long do you think that would take?"

"Don't know. It depends."

"On what?"

Not long, Malcolm thought, beginning perhaps by the end of the first or second session. "On the forces in the universe."

Winston nodded knowingly. "If you do a lousy job teaching music, you can always blame the forces in the universe."

Malcolm gave Winston a thumbs up. "Now you're catching on."

Malcolm noticed Winston's attitude changing even before Winston realized he had already begun the journey to fall in love with music. At first Winston complained he could not comprehend the relationship between notes and chords in a given key, whether major and minor, never mind how those related to other keys. "Who cares about the circle of fifths?" he snorted with less conviction than he may have intended.

Malcolm recalled how long it took him to understood how the circle of fifths applied to playing the clarinet. He regularly had to remind Winston, "What's our goal?"

"To simplify. Where now everything seems different and difficult, we want to boil it down, understanding, to where

WHEN THE SAINTS GO MARCHING IN

so much in music becomes familiar and easy." Winston then thrust his clarinet in the air as if once again he wanted to use it as a weapon. "Only, I don't see what that means, and I don't see how that's going to happen!"

At the beginning and end of every lesson, Malcolm would pick up his horn and lead Winston through jamming. "Okay, this one's in concert F, which is?"

Winston would generally contort his mouth while answering, "The key of G."

"We're gonna play some blues in the key of G, you ready?" When Winston nodded, Malcolm would begin to play, reminding Winston of what they were doing along the way. "The minor seventh in the C chord, feel free to feel it, it's a blue note, also the minor third in the tonic. It likes to be heard in blues. The minor seventh in G moves you sometimes back where you've been. Hear the minor seventh in D? The subdominant is bigger than the dominant in blues. Don't need to get there too quickly. It's good to let your fingers and your feelings tell you when and where to go. Okay, you got it. Now, the important thing, don't think about it, just listen to yourself and to me and go where your heart tells you to play."

Every day Arnold searched beyond silence. He knew the musical connection between Malcolm and Winston created a great diversion of hope for June, and on a different level, also for himself. Confined to a wheelchair, this new chance to develop his grandson's love for music in some way opened up the potential of joy and pushed it headlong into a legacy for the future.

Of course days were hard. Arnold had a hospice caregiver. June wanted to spend as many hours as possible by his side, he the love of her life, experiencing life together so powerful and giving. Even though she knew the truth of hospice and she had been instrumental in all they had planned, in her heart she could not fathom being without him.

June, Arnold's rock, he endured the frail nature of arriving in and disappearing out of reality, even with no dementia. Especially he regretted having to choose relief, when the pain brought on moments of despair. On occasion, he slept hours at a time. When he awoke and felt June's presence, he would postpone the pills and endure the pain so he and June could have a few more words together.

More than once he had awakened to the distant sound of dueling clarinets. Over time, he could distinguish differences in the way his grandson played his horn. He felt such joy when Winston sounded like he was, *really feeling it.*

Arnold congratulated himself for the change. As a consequence of observing how boring playing music had become for Winston, Arnold conjured the proposition to have Malcolm as a teacher. He and June had been friends of Tristan's, who used to live in Holwell, not far away from Stevenson. Arnold attended the same primary school, where as a child Malcolm came with Tristan to visit for a day or two. Also, together, June and Arnold both saw Malcolm in their local music club playing jazz some years later, when Malcolm happened to be visiting England again from his home in Monterey, California. June had requested 'Sweet Lorraine.' The way Malcolm played the tune showed he really loved music. Arnold and June had much fun including Malcolm in their circle, especially since, apparently, Malcolm had not recalled their earlier encounters and therefore had no idea of the relevance of these coincidences and plans. Tristan's friend had brought energy back into their grandson's life.

On his last day, Arnold had managed to open his eyes. His face expanded with love as he saw June.

She had been waiting beside him for several hours. He gave her a look. His lips moved without sound, "I love you and only you..." She had been dreading this day and she had been waiting for this day. She did not want to lose him and she wanted the suffering to stop for him. The Hospice nurse had told her he would not finish out the afternoon. She kissed him on the lips and the cheek and on the forehead. As she backed away, he mouthed a request. She nodded. She could not hold back the tears.

Malcolm had been teaching Winston for two months. He had grown to love Winston as if he were his own grandson. Also, he had met Arnold, who he found funny and brilliant. Arnold, even when in pain, could say something funny or profound and even manage a laugh. On every visit, Malcolm's admiration of Arnold grew. Talking with Arnold reminded Malcolm of previous conversations he had experienced with lifelong friends including promises made.

Winston knew soon he would lose his grandfather, because his parents had been visiting every day. He recalled how much he used to hate to play the clarinet. How that had changed! He had joy for music even with his heavy heart, now wearing a red and blue vest and a dashing beige sport coat, both given to him by Malcolm along with important perspectives about playing from the heart, then about living, and then about dying. In so many ways, Malcolm passed along mind-freeing information filling in some of the blanks for Winston.

Arnold heard their voices, a few words here and there, drifting in and out. Stories, personal with and about him. He lifted a finger.

June had been talking about Arnold and her on their way to Brighton shortly after they met, such a joyous recollection, but then she paused, Arnold's raised index finger, a sign they had agree upon the week before. A wave of sadness overcame June. She bent down and kissed Arnold again, on the forehead, on the cheeks, then on the lips.

"I love you. I will always love you," she said. She put her hand in his and knelt beside his bed. She nodded to Malcolm and Winston who put their clarinets to their lips.

Days later, while eating a homemade muffin at his neighbors, Winston explained as the clarity of the end came to him. "That meant he wanted to hear me, us, me and Malcolm, play. The song he chose, 'When the Saints Go Marching In.' Malcolm got it started kind of slow, and then he just gave it over and let me lead, and I just played what I felt, and then we went one time through. I looked at my grandmother, and she nodded for us to keep playing, so we played it a little faster, and then I had my eyes on my grandfather and I was feeling different and we played it a little slower, all kinds of different notes, and then I started crying, and finally I was crying so hard I couldn't play anymore and I just stopped, and my mom hugged me. My dad hugged me. My gram hugged me, and Malcolm softly, like a prayer, finished it off. And then my grandpa was gone."

Winston noticed his cheeks were wet with tears. "I've got to get home," he said.

June waited for Winston at the open front door. She had been crying as she thought about all the plans and fun Arnold and she had over the years. But now she glowed as she saw her grandson step toward her. "You made your grandfather so proud."

"Thanks Gram."

"And all of us, everybody else." They hugged for a long time. It had been both hard and fulfilling, with the funeral the day before. The house had bulged with close friends and well-wishers.

"Is Malcolm going to stick around so I can take more lessons?"

June turned her head upwards. In a silent communication, *What do you think, Arnold?* She hugged Winston.

"He's gone back to visit Tristan for a day or two, but he said, he'd be back to teach you more about music."

"Oh, good," said Winston.

Seeing the dreamy look on his gram's face, made him realize what he really wanted to do. "Gram, is it all right if I play 'When the Saints Go Marching In?'"

"Of course, my love."

"For grandpa. I think he'd like to hear it again."

His gram hugged him so tight. He hugged her back even tighter.

"I know that would mean more than anything to him."

Her words filled him with warmth and love and hope.

Staying in the cottage through the musical rebirth of a young boy and the death of his grandfather had brought Malcolm new love for all and a greater appreciation for Arnold and June's plan, including his continued adjunct support for Winston, a current June request and a previous Arnold promise. He filled out an application to extend his visa. For him the fates had interceded on his behalf one more time without any planning or requests and they had brought to him great gifts beyond his expectations.

A Flash In Time

Alice feared the ocean, even shore breaks barely crashing. Something more than courage enabled her to keep moving with her back to the surging tide. She pushed against Sean as he gazed longingly toward the large and growing surf and continued stepping toward hazard.

"You remember the desert, Sean, the extreme heat the last time we were there and what you said about the beach?" She glanced at loud squawking seagulls. He showed no sign of hearing them. His face seemed immune to listening.

The timber of her voice drifted like a whimper covered by the ocean's commerce. For a day with such warmth, the color of the water had filled with too much gray. Also, without billowing huge cheeks to even push a breeze, why had so many white caps topped off the enormous gurgling swells at Beer Can Beach?

Sean squinted. "I remember the desert. Flowers fighting to be seen through the dust. Lizards here and there, hiding under the rocks."

Alice grabbed Sean's shirt sleeve. "We saw a lot of lizards and bright beautiful yellow cactus flowers you juxtaposed to the threatening heat in your poems."

Sean lifted his nose. "And the mountains with our backs to the wind."

"I loved the way you wrote about the mountains."

"Their faces insurmountable. The wind that day. Blustery."

"Switchbacks. We could have made it to the top."

"There had been an avalanche..."

"No. That was earlier in the year, when the place was snowed in!" Aggravated, Alice bent the heal of her hand against his chest.

Sean glanced down, as if he had only now realized she had him by the shirt sleeve. "I remember the scent you wore that day. I wrote a poem about it."

She held him tighter and shook her head in exasperation. "We just can't go back to that."

"There's nowhere else to go."

"We've been there too many times."

In the distance, Sean observed a new set of waves forming and rolling. "*Exhilarating skies beyond sideways gusts of hailing sands...*"

His eyes seemed crazed. "I loved that poem of yours, Sean, but now we're here."

"One could see the yellow cactus flowers, *brightly teasing long-awaited rings of easy laughter....*"

"An even better line. So stop! When things are right, we laugh a lot, Sean."

"We have laughed a lot."

"And we can laugh so much more!"

"We can. I like laughing." Sean changed his weight from one foot to the other as if being pulled by the ocean.

With almost equal force Alice pushed her shoulder against him and took hold of his arm while keeping his sleeve. "Don't be stupid. I love you."

Sean nodded knowingly. "And you love the mountains along the desert."

"Come on, Sean, stop moving! I love you."

Now, Sean nudged his feet further through the sand. "I love you too." His mind seemed far off, as if beyond where he could see. "Today it's foggy, my memory of the desert."

"You need to fight for yourself and for us, Sean."

He shuffled into greater depth, steering her with his arm out of his way.

She forced herself to step back in an effort to block his movement. The water climbed against her back. "You said you would be better if we could get to the beach."

"In a manner of speaking, I am." He stepped slowly through the heavy churning.

Her grip weakened as deepening water lightened her footprint and triggered fear.

His eyes became hazy. "The sets of waves are getting larger. You can see what's coming against the sky."

As the high surf pulled her sideways, she grabbed him and hung on with both hands. Her feet would not follow his striding. A wave punched her, and he slipped from her grasp. Her legs shot out from under her. She summersaulted through turbulence and tumbled roughly losing her reference and unable to breathe, her eyes stinging, her lungs coughing, her fingers grappling through the water. Panic grabbed her and threw her into disequilibrium. Her cheek hit the sand and the undercurrents drew her toward the sea. She sank with sorrow and futility. In attempting to prevent her lover's death had she contributed to her own? She fought the urge to breath in water. She willed herself not to suck in water. She tightened the muscles in her neck, preventing her lungs from gasping. It took all her strength to finally relax and better observe the ocean's power. Had her mind begun to accept her fate? Suddenly, something grabbed her buttocks and pushed her through the whirling torrents to where she could finally gain a bit of breath. She clung to his head, still beneath the surface. Gasping with fear, she could feel the power of the whirling hungry rips wanting to devour everything. Coughing and gasping, having a hard time breathing, Sean continued to hold her high, as she now sat on his shoulder. He had his footing, and he pushed his feet slowly through the raging foam.

Finally, she began to feel safe. His look had changed, distance replaced by compassion, even love, he eased her lower, his arm wrapped around her waist. He held her close.

"I'm sorry," he said.

She wondered what that meant. She felt like punching him hard in the nose. Her father, a rancher in Carmel Valley where she had been raised, had warned her to stay away from Sean, the poet, such a mercurial, even if somewhat creative, loser.

Now Sean spoke, full of empathy and remorse. "I wouldn't blame you if you told me to go to hell."

Her words came out slowly and distinctly. "Go to hell." The waves had turned them so they faced the horizon. She scanned the white water and beyond. As peculiar as it seemed to her at the time, for some reason she remembered she had not been wearing any scent on the day in question and neither had he.

The squawking seagulls had silenced their calls.

She caught a glimpse of a large pelican up high suddenly brake flight, pull back wings, and dive deep like a spear. She watched it streak along a line and disappear with a snap into the ocean's skin.

ABOOKS

ALIVE Book Publishing and ALIVE Publishing Group
are imprints of Advanced Publishing LLC,
3200 A Danville Blvd., Suite 204, Alamo, California 94507

Telephone: 925.837.7303
alivebookpublishing.com

www.ingramcontent.com/pod-product-compliance
Lightning Source LLC
Chambersburg PA
CBHW030131260626
47156CB00008B/2897